The tw

each other, t... ... ...
nacelle bumping the gondola of the Prussian airship and sending it swinging out of the way. The
side of the gondola scraped against the airbag
like fingernails against a blackboard.

Tom winced, hoping desperately that it wasn't
the sound of the stiff fabric of the nacelle ripping open.

The zeppelin's gondola, bristling with Gatling
guns and cannon, hove into view, swinging like
a pendulum, dark smoke belching from its
stack. Tom watched a hapless Prussian airman
fall from his station and over the side. At this
altitude, he was a goner.

Suddenly, the Prussian ship rolled without
warning, and the hull of the aerobattleship and
the gondola of the zeppelin slammed together,
locking in an embrace of distressed metal.

FROM PRUSSIA
WITH LOVE

FROM PRUSSIA WITH LOVE

A Castle Falkenstein™ Novel

by

John DeChancie

PRIMA PUBLISHING

ISBN: 1-55958-772-5
Library of Congress Catalog Card Number: 94-080150
Printed in the United States of America
95 96 97 98 EE 10 9 8 7 6 5 4 3 2 1

PROLOGUE

Let me tell you a story about a king named Ludwig. Ludwig was king in a world of Faerie and romance, a world that isn't our world but looks much like it on the surface.

But first, Ludwig was a real king in our world. He was born in a part of Germany called Bayern, or Bavaria, as most people call it, a land of majestic mountains and lush countryside, in the year 1845. His father, King Maximilian II, died when Ludwig was eighteen years old, and Ludwig succeeded to the throne. The young king was a sensitive, shy, introverted, poetic man who enjoyed an extremely rich fantasy life.

He loved music, especially the music of Richard Wagner. He loved mythology, especially that of the Teutonic past.

Known both as the Dream King and the Swan King, he fancied himself a medieval knight on a sacred quest for a Holy Grail known only to him. He was something of an enigma, as much to himself as to others. He loved to build grand castles, built many, and dreamed of building even grander ones.

Ludwig was not a practical man and often erred on the side of profligacy in financial matters. He fought constantly with his ministers of state and ultimately warred with them over his very throne.

It is said that he descended into madness. Indeed that was the charge his ministers made in their attempt to unseat him. At first they failed, but in time they succeeded. Ludwig was declared insane and held in custody while an appointed Regent acted as head of state.

Ludwig ended badly, drowing in a boating accident (some called it suicide) on 13 June, 1886.

But that, happily, is not the end of the story; rather it is the beginning of one. Because Ludwig did not really drown in that accident. Faerie hands plucked him from this reality and set him down gently in another world, the world of New Europa. New Europa was Europe, but vastly transformed—the sort of Europe where dragons were as common as jetliners are in our world.

It was Auberon, High Lord of the Seelie Court, who orchestrated Ludwig's rescue. With the help of many—humans, dwarfs, and even a man from our world (we'll get to him soon), Auberon succeeded in restoring Ludwig to the throne of New Europa's Bayern, where he ruled more wisely, sanely, and pragmatically than he had in his previous life. The best part: he built the grandest castle of them all, Castle Falkenstein.

Why did Auberon do all this? Why did he transport Ludwig to New Europa? Well, that is what our story is all about—a tale of Castle Falkenstein.

Now, we begin.

CHAPTER 1

THE ROCKETS
OF PRUSSIA

Thunder clapped in the sky and the crew on the bridge of the aeroship looked up.

Tom Olam knew that the thick white contrail racing across the blue belonged to a rocket even before he heard the surprised exclamations of the aeroship's crew. A rocket was the only thing it could be. And of course the thunder was easily explained.

A sonic boom.

"What in blazes is that thing up there?" said the aeroship's skipper, Captain Karlheinz Jäger, who stood at Tom's shoulder.

"A ballistic missile."

"What?"

"A rocket."

Thomas Edward Olam was the only crew member of the aeroship *Richard Wagner* who knew what a ballistic missile was, because he was the only man aboard who had seen one. He had seen them in the twentieth century, in a different universe.

Still craning his neck, the ship's first officer was incredulous. "Captain Olam . . . I mean no disrespect, but a rocket? An artillery rocket?"

"Amazing," Tom said as he watched the thing's trajectory bend toward the Baltic sea.

Tom was amazed for a number of reasons. The chief one was that the rocket was wildly anachronistic. This was Europe (or as it was called in this continuum, New Europa), in the Year of Our Lord 1872. The thing streaking across the sky at supersonic speed could not . . . *could not* . . . be a jet or rocket-propelled aircraft. Heavier-than-air aviation had not yet been developed. Even if it secretly had been, you could not jump from Wright-brothers-style powered gliders to supersonic flight in anything less than decades. Therefore, that rapidly receding metal cylinder up there, trailing an enormously thick and puffy contrail (Tom wondered about that) had to be a ballistic rocket. Rockets had existed for centuries, and someone, even the stodgy and conservative Prussians, could have been experimenting with them.

Tom felt also a sense of foreboding, because not far from here, on the coast, lay a quiet, out-of-the-way fishing village.

Peenemünde. The very name reverberated. "Ye gods, so soon?"

The Unseelie were doing their best to heat up the pace of technological development in this universe. Why? No doubt they had their extremely obscure, if not incomprehensible, reasons. Obscure and incomprehensible because the Unseelie, led by the demonic Adversary, weren't human. They were Faerie.

Opposed to them were other Faerie, in an alliance with humans, dwarfs, and dragons: the Second Compact. Tom had been instrumental in forging that alliance.

"Couldn't be liquid-fueled," Tom muttered. "Couldn't be!"

"What was that, Captain Olam?" Jäger was frowning at him.

"Nothing. Captain Jäger, I strongly recommend we try to find where that thing comes down."

Jäger smiled wryly. "As this is an intelligence mission, I will take your 'strong recommendation,' which you doubtless wish were an order. Is there a chance it didn't come from the Prussians?"

Tom shrugged. "Not much of one."

Jäger turned. "Airman Schultz!"

"Yes, Herr Captain?"

"Still have your eye on it?"

"Yes, Herr Captain!"

"Good. Try to get a fix on where it hits the sea."

"Yes, Herr Captain."

"Helm! Come about ninety degrees, north."

The first officer relayed the order to the helmsman, who threw the huge rudder-controled wheel hard to the left. The aeroship neatly executed a sharp left turn, banking gently.

"Full speed ahead!"

Tom had a sudden thought. Maybe it had been a meteorite. Meteorites could take on strange appearances, even

leave contrails. Many a UFO report in the twentieth century
had at its bottom an exotic meteorite sighting.

No. Though it had been little more than a dot against the
sky, Tom had seen the shape clearly: a metallic cylinder, a big
one, tapered gracefully. The damned contraption had looked
for all the world like a V-2. How could this be?

Ye gods, maybe it *had* been a UFO.

Not possible. The notion of gray, almond-eyed aliens in
this Age of Steam was extravagantly incongruous. Just why
this was so, he couldn't figure. Yes, he could. Damn it, aliens
just didn't fit. Not in this magic-ridden time and place. Space
aliens belonged in the hard-science universes, which were
few and far between out there in the multitudes of continua
beyond the Faerie Veil.

Besides, weren't the Seelie and Unseelie spooks enough? To
say nothing of goblins, sprites, kobolds, leprechauns, and
unicorns, among many, many other unearthly creatures. This
was such a *cluttered* world, supernaturally speaking.

"You have the conn, Herr Wendt," Jäger told his first
officer. "Continue the search while reducing altitude
steadily." He then signaled Tom to follow, and both headed to
the chart room. The navigator was busy on the bridge taking
magnetic compass readings, and a corresponding chart was
laid out on the table. Tom and Jäger studied it. There were
no nearby islands.

"Whoever launched the rocket wasn't aiming at anything
in particular," Tom ventured.

"It was meant to crash into the open sea?" Jäger asked.

"Yes. Rockets aren't recoverable, usually. With any luck,
this is an early test of a prototype. They're probably surprised it worked at all."

Tom decided to believe himself and breathed a little easier. But he couldn't help thinking: my God, what if they have a guidance system?

"Could they have been aiming for Sweden?"

"That would be an act of war," Tom said. "Besides, the Swedish coast is a hundred or more kilometers away. The thing's range was obviously limited. Which is good. With a guidance system and a respectable range, it'd be all but operational."

"Guidance system?" Jäger said.

"A mechanism to direct the missile's flight to its target."

"The thought of a *guided* missile is most disquieting," Jäger said.

"'Guided missile' is exactly what we are talking about here, Captain Jäger."

Hoping that he was merely being an alarmist, Tom followed the aeroship's skipper out of the chart room and back onto the bridge.

Airman Schultz pointed out to sea. "There, Herr Captain."

"Keep your eye on the spot," Jäger instructed.

"Sea vessel off to starboard," the first officer announced. "Fishing boat."

"Doubt they're doing any fishing," Tom said. "Observers."

Maybe the crash point had been planned after all. Worrisome. Though the boat could have just been lucky enough to be at the right place at the right time.

The giant Bavarian airship swooped over the fishing boat. Men stood on its decks, looking up. They did not resemble fishermen.

The boat receded into the distance as the aeroship pressed on. Ahead, a curious plume of white steam rose from the surface. Around the plume, the sea bubbled.

"Take her down," the captain ordered.

"Yes, Herr Captain!"

"That's where it hit," Olam said, pointing. "Steam. The damn thing had a steam engine!"

Tom laughed to himself. He should have known. Even advanced solid-fuel rocketry would have been a bit much for the nineteenth century. But steam? This was the Age of Steam.

There wasn't much to inspect at the crash site. Not much of the wreckage could float. There were a few chunks of something, though. Rubber, it looked like, or cork, maybe. Gaskets? Bushing? It was hard to tell. Along with them, a small grayish white object bobbed in the water. A bit of wadding or insulation, perhaps.

Olam pointed at it. "Can you make that out?" he asked the captain.

Jäger squinted. "Where?"

"There."

"Not quite," Jäger said. "Take her down, Commander! All the way to the surface. Raise the rudder!"

Orders were shouted and relayed. On the lower decks, airmen manned the crank that controlled the deployment of the aeroship's steering rudder. The huge aerodynamic structure, a cross between a vertical wing and the grip of a pistol, retracted into its landing position, parallel to the direction of flight.

The surface of the sea came up fast.

"I'm going below," Tom said, and made for a hatch. Scrambling down a series of ladders, he descended to the lowest deck of the aeroship and went out to the narrow walkway.

The plume was dead ahead, the surface of the sea not ten meters below. Still, the ship descended.

The white object bobbed in the bubbling water directly below. It looked strange.

Puzzled, Tom shook his head just as the ship's landing wheel dipped into the water. The drag caused a sudden deceleration that shoved Tom against the rail, but he held on, still scrutinizing the floating white thing.

It was . . . no, this is silly.

A bird. A dead bird.

A . . . seagull? No.

A pigeon. A white pigeon.

"What the hell?" Stumped, Tom searched his mind. There was no doubt that the bird had been a passenger on the rocket.

Space travel? Had the Prussians gone space-happy all of a sudden? What were they doing, trying to put the world's first space satellite into orbit almost a century ahead of schedule?

Someone shouted from an upper deck—one of the lookouts screamed a warning. Tom looked up and drew a quick breath.

A Prussian dirigible, a zeppelin, was closing fast, at about a thousand feet.

Fighting the g-forces of the ship's rapid rise, Tom climbed all the way back to the bridge, breathing heavily as he arrived. He scanned the sky. A second zeppelin was closing off the starboard bow. What they were trying to do was obvious. Positioning themselves directly in the *Wagner*'s path, they were playing chicken, daring the Bavarian aeroship to ram them.

While the zeppelins were no technological match for an aerobattleship of the Bavarian aeronavy, they now had an altitude advantage. If they wanted to open up on the *Wagner*, they could inflict severe, even fatal, damage.

But Bavaria and Prussia were not at war. Chances were the zeppelin's skipper would not fire unless fired upon.

But you could never tell about Prussians. Ruled by militarists, they relished a good dust up. Prussia claimed these waters, though not many of her neighbors recognized the greedy grab of so much sea.

"Herr Captain, shall we level off?" the first officer asked nervously.

"Dump number two ballast tank! Continue the ascent at maximum acceleration!"

A Bavarian aerobattleship boasted two advantages over a zeppelin: speed, provided by its powerful top-secret magnetic engine, and altitude, supplied by the terrific pressure inside its non burning hydrogen gas nacelle. Dwarf technology accounted for the exotic material of the gas nacelle, which provided extra pressure and lifting power. Seelie sorcery had produced the noninflammable hydrogen (known as helium in any other universe).

A Prussian shell hit the sea far off the bow. The second ship had fired a shot without remotely intending to hit anything. Purely a warning. The first had disappeared from view, blocked by the *Wagner*'s gas nacelle.

"Herr Captain," the first officer exclaimed, "the Prussian is directly overhead!"

"We'll see if he has any mettle to back up his intimidation. Continue ascent to two thousand feet!"

Tom gripped the rail, leaning out precariously to look over the upper rim of the gas nacelle.

A shout reached them, amplified by some non-electronic device. It was doubtless the zeppelin's skipper, ordering the *Wagner* to level off in a sibilant Prussian accent.

Captain Jäger was having none of it.

"Herr Captain, we're about to collide!"

"He'll get the worst of it," Jäger said calmly.

The two airships came up against each other, the upper surface of the *Wagner*'s nacelle bumping the gondola of the Prussian airship and sending it swinging out of the way. The side of the gondola scraped against the airbag like fingernails against a blackboard.

Tom winced, hoping desperately that it wasn't the sound of the stiff fabric of the nacelle ripping open.

The zeppelin's gondola, bristling with Gatling guns and cannon, hove into view, swinging like a pendulum, dark smoke belching from its stack. Tom watched a hapless Prussian airman fall from his station and over the side. At this altitude, he was a goner.

Suddenly, the Prussian ship rolled without warning, and the hull of the aerobattleship and the gondola of the zeppelin slammed together, locking in an embrace of distressed metal.

Tom soared over the rail and into space. He fell only a short distance, however, before landing flat on his back on metal. Unhurt, he sat up quickly, then struggled to get to his feet.

He was astonished to find himself on the outer observation deck of the Prussian airship, lying up against the hull, as the deck was tilted sharply.

"Uh . . . hi, there."

A Prussian officer held a small multi-barrelled "pepper-box" revolver on him.

"Hauptmann!" Tom said, recognizing him. "As I live and breathe, Rupert Hauptmann. Of the Prussian Imperial Service, if I'm not mistaken."

The man's thin lips curled into a smirk as debonair as it was evil. His hair was a shock of brown over a narrow forehead and thick brows. His eyes were a cold, grayish blue, the blue of gun metal and bruises. "Captain Thomas Olam! I'd been hoping we'd meet again."

"Sorry for just dropping by," Tom said, with a grin. "Can't stay, though. Must dash off—toodles."

"You're going nowhere. So happy to have you aboard, Olam. Though you won't be here long." Hauptmann's insincere smile crinkled the long, ugly dueling scar on his right cheek.

"Sorry, am I interrupting something?"

"Not at all. It's simply that I'm going to kill you right now."

The Prussian cocked the pistol, but a sudden pitch of the deck sent the man lurching against Tom, who simply raised a knee. The knee connected all too well, and Hauptmann's face screwed up in surprise and pain. The pistol dropped and so did the Prussian.

"Ewwww, I bet that hurt," Tom said sympathetically.

Again, suddenly, the world became very disorienting. Metal bent with hideous groaning, and the two ships' hulls scrabbled at each other, whumping and banging, in a desperate attempt to separate. Tom looked over to where Hauptmann had lain, but he was gone.

Tom leaped up on the rail, held on to an upright, and tried to distinguish the tangled wreckage—bent gun barrels, warped rail, flapping bulkhead—of one ship from that of the other. What he believed to be the lower deck of the *Wagner* hove past. If he didn't jump now, he could look forward to the possibility of permanent imprisonment aboard the Prussian air dreadnought . . . or worse.

The world fell out from under him. The gondola of the dirigible, its suspension members sheared or strained beyond limit, separated from its cigar-shaped bag and fell toward the sea, spilling men and wreckage in a gruesome, fragmented shower.

Tom floated in space, curiously suspended between the blue of heaven and the darker blue of the sea. A length of hawser whipped past him, and he reached for it.

His hands caught fire, the rope burning through them like a red-hot snake. He managed to halt his slide, and there he hung, like a sandbag on a loose mooring tether, almost a thousand feet above the sea. He looked down.

The Prussian gondola struck the water, sending up a towering fountain of foam.

Not very survivable, that crash, Tom thought.

"Whoa, wait a minute."

What the hell was that, floating gently toward the sea? A big yellow and orange lozenge-shaped rubbery thing, with something dangling under it. A balloon, maybe? Tom blinked. Just some bit of equipment from the dirigible. An inflatable raft, wafting down uselessly.

The hawser's turning took the mysterious apparition out of his field of vision. No time now to wonder. More pressing was the question of whether or not he would have the strength to climb up to the aeroship.

He looked down. The other zeppelin was at least two hundred meters below the *Wagner* now, and far to stern. She would never catch her prey.

He looked up. Heavily damaged, but more or less intact and operational, the *Wagner* was still climbing. Freed of its encumbering weight, the gasbag of the downed zeppelin was already a dot in the sky. It would continue to rise until it burst in the thin air of the upper atmosphere. Everything was okay.

Except for the little problem of climbing back up to the ship.

Tom couldn't decide what troubled him the most: His present predicament, the Prussian rocket, or the fact that he had neatly precipitated a serious international incident.

Combination of the three, he decided.

CHAPTER 2

THE THREAT

Cabinet Secretary Franz von Pfistermeister, confidential aide to the King of Bayern (in some quarters of the globe better known as Bavaria), saw Rhyme Enginemaster coming toward him along one of Castle Falkenstein's pink marble hallways and quickly debated the best course of action. Rhyme had a reputation for rudeness. Was it better to acknowledge the ugly, diminutive dwarf or simply ignore him and let him pass? There was danger in either course. Although dwarfs liked to keep to themselves and ordinarily shunned the amenities, Rhyme was quite capable of taking offense at a snub, especially one from a minister so close to King Ludwig.

Strange little creatures, Pfistermeister mused, quite intelligent for all their misshapen bodies. They weren't human. Dwarfs were another race, another species entirely.

"Good morning, Rhyme!" Pfistermeister said in a booming voice that he instantly regretted. *Ach!* poured it on a bit thick, didn't?

"What's good about it?" Rhyme halted his progress down the rococo corridor. Dropping his wooden toolbox with a thump, he stared up at the tall, thin official.

"Uh . . . well . . . actually, as a matter of fact—" Pfistermeister adjusted his pince-nez, a bit irked. Who was this gnarled, repulsive creature to show such effrontery to the King's most confidential minister? Look at him. Frazzle-haired and bearded, about the height of a hitching post, the dwarf wore baggy blue coveralls vented with far too many pockets, all of them bristling with hammers, wrenches, and other tools. He presented a comical figure bottomed out by those absurdly big workboots.

However, the safety and welfare of Ludwig's realm sometimes turned on the doings of this improbable creature in his workshop deep in the bowels of Castle Falkenstein. That was unsettling to Pfistermeister. Yet it was true.

And, as it was true, the creature must be accorded deference. To a certain extent. "How . . . uh, goes it down in your workshop?"

"How goes what?" The dwarf squinted one emerald green eye suspiciously.

Pfistermeister shrugged. "Whatever it is you're working on at the moment."

"I'm not working on anything at the moment, if you're referring to one of your ridiculous requests."

"What requests?"

"The silly suggestions for research projects that you and the rest of your long-coated colleagues throw out, wanting me to come up with magic formulas for unbreakable swords, rifles that never need reloading, wagon axles that never break. Nonsense."

"What's wrong with any of that?" Pfistermeister said irritably. "Any one of those things would help His Majesty's armed forces meet the Prussian threat."

"Addle-brained nonsense. You want miracles. I don't deal in miracles."

"We don't expect miracles," Pfistermeister objected. "Anything would be better than those silly infernal gadgets of yours that never seem to work."

Rhyme's eyes flashed. "Silly gadgets, eh? Why, you scrawny beanstalk, I'm working on something now that will make you eat those words! Then you will see a miracle!"

Pfistermeister sniffed. "Indeed?"

"Indeed," Rhyme shot back.

"And what is it?"

"None of your damned business, that's what!"

The dwarf picked up his toolbox and stalked off down the opulent rococo hallway, big boots clomping along the pink marble floor.

"You had best stick to your proper function in this castle," Pfistermeister called after him. "Sewers, water pipes, drains. You know, looking after the plumbing!"

"Ram the plumbing up your bum!" Rhyme yelled over his shoulder.

"Really!" Pfistermeister's back fairly arched with indignation. "Unspeakable little monster!"

As the dwarfish figure plodded down the hallway, Pfistermeister fought for composure. He had gambled and had lost. He resolved never again to speak to a dwarf. Any dwarf.

Remembering that he was late for an important meeting with the king, Pfistermeister hurried in the other direction. One question nettled him.

Exactly what miracle was Rhyme Enginemaster working on?

"As you are attending a conference on matters military, sire, I should think the general's uniform the most appropriate."

"You really think so, Fritz? I'm of two minds about parading about like some tin soldier today."

Fritz, King Ludwig's personal valet, rolled his eyes. "Whatever is your wish, sire. But this is the only outfit ready to wear. If you desire another, you will have to wait for the cleaners and pressers."

"Bother. Never mind, this will do."

Ludwig Wittelsbach of Bayern, king by the Grace of God, stepped back from the mirror to take in his costume's full effect. It was one of majestic simplicity. The tunic was of baby blue wool with silver buttons, the breast crossed with a magenta sash. A gold chain with squared jeweled links swung from his shoulders, supporting a medallion—a Maltese cross inscribed with a swimming swan.

Smooth white riding breeches were stuffed into knee-high black patent leather boots. A golden scabbard hung from a silvered belt, the golden hilt of his sword gleaming above it.

"There he is," the king said. "Ludovicus II. *Rex Bavariae*."

"Pardon, sire?"

"The Latin inscription on my sword. You see, right here? Never mind."

Fritz took two steps back and stood at attention.

The king continued eying himself. He was still a young man, dark-haired, neatly bearded, handsome. He knew it and liked it.

"I suppose this will do. Now, the royal cape."

From the armoire, Fritz fetched a floor-length cape lined in ermine and studded with little black-tipped tails. A lot of animals had died to make this garment. He draped it over the monarch's shoulders.

The effect was impressive.

"Thank you, Fritz, that will be all, I think. Oh, the gloves."

White satin gloves completed the look.

"Good."

Ludwig clicked his boot heels together.

"I am ready for the meeting." The king sighed. "I have little heart for matters of state today. I'd rather take a day trip to Hohenschwangau and watch swans on the Alpsee."

"They are beautiful creatures," Fritz commented.

"Yes, they are." The king absently fingered the medallion. "I often wonder what attracts me to them."

"Perhaps, sire, it's because you and they are . . . alike in some way."

"Ugly ducklings, perhaps."

"Sire?"

"The nursery story of the ugly duckling. You know. It was really a swan . . ." The king turned from the mirror. "Let it pass. Make sure my formal suit is ready for the ball this evening."

"Yes, sire. The seamstress has it now and she should have it ready for pressing by three o'clock."

"Satisfactory. Now to business."

Leaving his dressing room, King Ludwig strode through his royal apartments, a succession of eclectic and lavishly decorated rooms. He cut through a Moorish sitting room to a French provincial parlor, and left that to walk through the immense Italian dining room where the walls shimmered with elaborate murals. Pausing, he gazed wistfully at a view of Tannhäuser in Venusburg, a city given over exclusively to the senses.

"*Ach,*" the king said sadly, then moved on.

If only fantasy were reality. The mural and the wonderful *myth* it depicted represented for him something lost, never to be regained, as if it were in a past life he still felt its siren call.

At last, he came to two broad white-lacquered doors emblazoned with the royal seal. A liveried servant drew them apart and the king stepped into a spacious private conference room with a huge circular table at its center. The pine top of the round table held scenes inlaid in fruitwoods showing the life of King Arthur, with each tableau enwreathed in runic inscriptions of elaborate Celtic symbology. It was a stunning piece of workmanship. The rest of the room looked darkly Teutonic; the walls were hung with ancient shields, coats of arms, and medieval tapestries.

Rising from the table to greet the king were Pfistermeister, Colonel Rudolph von Tarlenheim in full dress uniform, and Morrolan the wizard. With them was the foreigner Captain Thomas Edward Olam, the man who talked as though he were from another time . . . another world entirely. This morning, Olam's face was grim, as were all their faces. King Ludwig felt his stomach shift unpleasantly.

"Gentlemen," he said. "Be seated."

"Good morning, Your Majesty," Pfistermeister said.

"Good morning, Herr Cabinet Secretary. I trust it will still be a good morning after I am apprised of the grave situation which required this secret meeting."

"'Grave' is not exactly the word for the situation, Your Majesty," Tarlenheim said. "I would say that what we have to tell you is a matter of some concern for the near future. But it does not represent an immediate threat. At least, we don't think so."

"Good." The king seated himself in the chair with the highest back. There was, of course, no position at the round table that could be called the head of the table. However, the king always sat in the chair clearly reserved for a first among equals. "What do you have for me, Gentlemen?"

"Rockets, Your Majesty?" Tom Olam replied. He glanced at the others. "I thought we'd get right to the point, if there's no objection."

The king's bushy brows drew together. "Rockets?"

"Yes," Colonel Tarlenheim said. "Military rockets."

"What about them?" Ludwig was enjoying the conference less all the time.

The colonel leaned forward. "They are in fact what precipitated the incident with the Prussian airship, of which I informed His Majesty this morning."

"Dreadful affair," the king said. "I regret any loss of life, though all of it befell our adversaries. How did rockets precipitate it, Colonel?"

"Our aeroship, the one involved in the incident, observed a rocket directly before encountering the Prussian, sire.

Captain Olam, along with others aboard the *Wagner*, observed a giant rocket of a radically new type."

The colonel's mouth took on grim lines. "The Prussians are contriving new ways of using rockets for military purposes. Sir, I do not speak of garden-variety barrage rockets of the Congreve sort. Those have been part and parcel of military ordnance since the beginning of the century. Effective under some conditions, true, but usually more trouble than they're worth. They fly all over the damned place. There's no controlling them. These contraptions Bismarck is having built are different."

It was difficult for Ludwig to imagine a more difficult or unpleasant subject. The obvious tension in the others was catching, however, and he tried to keep his attention from wandering.

"These rockets are lots bigger, for one thing," Tom Olam said, tugging at his gloves under the table. Inside, they felt a bit icky, since his hands were covered with ointment for the rope burns. Rope burns were nothing to the fate he faced before Jäger's crew managed to haul him into the gondola.

"Yes, and they have a revolutionary new propulsion system." The colonel's voice vibrated with concern.

"When I first saw the thing overhead," Olam went on, "I thought for sure someone over there had stumbled onto liquid fuel technology. But that turns out not to be the case."

The king furrowed his forehead, wondering how long this meeting would run on. "What in the world is liquid fuel technology?"

"Sorry," Olam said. "I'm being anachronistic again. It's hard not to be, sometimes. What I'm talking about is an elaborate engine that mixes volatile chemicals and burns them to produce the thrust that drives the rocket. Such things will have to wait for another half century or two before mechanical engineering is up to the task. You'll need some other kinds of engineering along with it.

"But never mind. These Prussian rockets seem to be run by steam." The king's eyes appeared to be glazing over. Tom put more emphasis into his voice. "I didn't believe that, at first, because steam rocket technology is also for a future time. The main problem is in constructing a boiler chamber strong enough to withstand great internal pressures, yet light enough to be propelled by the exhaust the boiler produces. That's a thorny strength of materials problem, but it can be solved here and now, I think, if you steal a bit of the lightweight wizardry that went into our aeronavy ships."

"Obviously, some of our wizardry leaked," Colonel Tarlenheim said in a dour tone that at last drew the king's attention.

Pfistermeister asked, "What precisely do we know about the Prussian rocket project?"

"Not much," Tom answered. "We do know of a man in Prussia who has been writing about rockets for the last thirty years. His name is von Bremen. Karl Friedrich von Bremen. A scientist, though he hasn't many credentials. He has the reputation of being something of a crank, as well as a rocketry enthusiast."

The colonel said, "I hadn't known there were such people. But we have some information on von Bremen. He spent his life and part of his family's fortune building outlandish contraptions and shooting them off, sometimes scaring the neighbors half to death."

"He's been petitioning the Prussian government for years to fund research into advanced rocketry," Olam went on. "Been turned down pretty much across the board. But someone at an army artillery research lab must have run across his ideas and melded them with the lightweight materials stuff that just came through the spy pipeline. The result is a steam rocket engine that works."

"We believe von Bremen has been hired as an advisor," the colonel said. "We also know he has a laboratory and workshop on his family estate on the Baltic coast."

"And," Tom said, "we know that Rupert Hauptmann had something to do with the project."

"Hauptmann," Pfistermeister said sourly. "That black-guard! Er . . . 'had'?"

"We believe he perished in the crash of the airship," Tarlenheim told him.

"Good riddance, I say! If His Majesty will pardon me."

The king shrugged. "An evil man if ever there was one. Just deserts, I'd say." Sitting back, he crossed his legs. "All very interesting, gentlemen, but if you'll forgive me, I'm having trouble understanding much of this. Why should I be so concerned about a new kind of artillery piece? I realize a new weapon is always a threat, but all this technical detail is quite beyond my expertise, and in fact, quite beyond my interest."

The men exchanged glances. Each of them knew that their king's gentle nature could lead to the terrible destruction of his kingdom.

"Forgive me, sire," Pfistermeister said with tension beneath his gentle tone. "From what the colonel and Captain Olam have told me, this new machinery represents an entirely different kind of threat to your realm. I urge you to listen to what they have to say."

His epaulets shook as the king shrugged. "If they must speak, they must speak. Please continue, Colonel, Captain Olam."

"Thank you, sire," the colonel said. "The threat, as we see it, comprises two different possibilities. One is purely in the nature of, as you put it, sire, a new artillery piece. But one with an extremely long range. Longer, potentially, than the Verne Cannon."

"Rockets already have the Verne Cannon beat on two counts," Olam put in. "First, the Verne is a stationary weapon, and as such, its position can be overrun."

He knew he risked losing the king's interest with technical detail, but it was essential that Ludwig understand the peril facing his kingdom. "Also," Tom said, putting intensity into his voice, "the Verne is vulnerable to aerial bombardment. Rockets can be launched from mobile automotive carriers or even carted around in horse-drawn wagons and launched in the field. They can be extremely mobile weapons.

He tried to convey his deep concern to the monarch through an intense gaze. "Second, while the Verne can deliver a heavy shell a long distance, an intermediate-range rocket missile can deliver an even bigger warhead the same distance, or even farther. One strike on Castle Falkenstein could cause extensive damage."

"And, of course, a barrage of such projectiles," the colonel put in, "could reduce a city to ruins." He clenched his fists on the table. "Munich is vulnerable to this catastrophic weapon."

Clearly distressed, the king asked, "How many civilians, how many innocent women and children, would die in such an attack?"

"Thousands, perhaps, sire," Colonel Tarlenheim said.

"Shameful." Ludwig swiped one gloved hand across his forehead. "Such atrocities cannot be permitted in a Christian civilization."

"Nevertheless, sire," the colonel warned, "the Iron Chancellor means to threaten us with them. At the least, he'll hold their existence over our heads."

"Despicable," the king muttered.

"Indeed."

"You said there were two possibilities," the king reminded Tarlenheim.

"Yes, sire. The other is more in the nature of a threat to our new aeronavy. Captain Olam knows more about that than I do."

"Thanks, Colonel Tarlenheim," Olam said. "This is not an immediate threat, but if research and development continue along the line I anticipate, at the end of one road lies an anti-aerial missile. This represents a threat to our entire fleet of air dreadnoughts. They could be shot out of the sky by ground-based mobile missile batteries. Of course, there is the question of guidance, both with the city-smashing rockets and the anti-aerial kind."

"Guidance?" the king repeated, again sounding overwhelmed by the technical side of the matter.

"Yes, sire," Tom said urgently. "The mechanism for guiding the weapon to its target. As the colonel pointed out, rockets have a tendency to fly all over the place. They're notoriously hard to control. That's why they still remain an adjunct to the world's artillery forces. They're a bit undependable. But with a proper internal guidance system, a rocket missile becomes a deadly accurate device. The problem, of course, amounts to coming up with an analytical engine that can fit inside a rocket and not weigh a ton."

The king rubbed his dark eyebrows. "I'm sorry, I've lost the train of thought. Now we're talking about analytical engines. How do these relate to rocket weapons?"

"Theoretically," Tom said, choosing words the monarch would understand, "an analytical engine could be programmed to guide a rocket weapon to its target. Without it, the rocket would have only a minimal chance of hitting its mark. But weight and size are big problems. Analytical engines tend to weigh a ton, and they're bulky as the dickens."

"I see," the king said. "Rockets, analytical engines, threats, death. Destruction." He heaved a great sigh. "Why is it always thus?"

Again, the men exchanged worried glances. Ludwig was a good man, but if he could not be convinced to act, his country would be imperiled.

"The world does not change, sire," the colonel said. "The bellicose human beast, the creature that burnt the topless towers of Troy, is the same one who makes war today."

"I fear that is true," the king lamented. "*Ach*. But what can one monarch do?"

"We can counter the threat." The colonel spoke with absolute conviction.

Ludwig regarded him warily. "How so?"

"By instituting a rocket research program of our own."

The king's dark brows shot up. "What?"

"Sire, it is the only way."

Ludwig thumped a fist on the tabletop, his handsome features darkening. "I'll not have it! Colonel, I will not be responsible for the deaths of thousands. Such weapons of mass destruction could lead to the end of civilization as we know it."

"This all sounds very familiar," Tom Olam said more or less to himself, but drawing a dubious look from Pfistermeister. Inside, his heart was sinking.

"There is danger in such an undertaking," Colonel Tarlenheim conceded. "But what are we to do, sire? Are we to let Bismarck blackmail us? Are we to let him gain a monopoly on these weapons?" The colonel's voice shook with passion. "We might as well cede our country right now and be done with it."

"Surely, you overstate the situation," the king suggested.

Tarlenheim's eyes flashed. "We will have absolutely no defense against rocket attack. Our cities will fall. We will be helpless to defend them."

The king folded his hands on the table, brooding. "I cannot in good conscience cause such diabolical plans to be undertaken. No. No, it cannot be."

Pfistermeister said, "Sire, I fear it must be."

The colonel turned to the wizard. "Morrolan, you haven't said a word yet. What do you think of all this? Is there any sorcery behind this rocket business?"

Morrolan had been sitting back, listening attentively, a faint smile on his face.

Shifting position, he recrossed his legs. The smile broadened a bit. "Sorcery? Why, of course there's sorcery behind it."

Tarlenheim slapped the table. "Then we need sorcery to counter it!"

"Begging your pardon, Colonel," Tom said, "but I don't agree."

Tarlenheim was on uncertain ground. This engineer's talk was annoying him. He decided to defer to someone who knew what he was talking about. "We don't need sorcery?"

"We need technology," Tom said. "Rocket technology. Fast."

Tarlenheim shrugged. "Where would we get it?"

"I have an idea," Tom said. "Marianne's at the Vatican, isn't she?"

"Yes," Tarlenheim said, confused.

"I suggest we get off a wire ordering her to Florence. She should look up a fireworks magnate by the name of Ruggiero Zambelli."

Dubious, Tarlenheim repeated, "Fireworks?"

"Yes. Zambelli is something of a rocket enthusiast, the only one in the world outside Prussia. If anyone can persuade him to join us, Marianne can."

"Fireworks," the king said absently. "Interesting. Distasteful as I find the military applications of this matter, I must admit that some aspects of it intrigue me." For a moment he drifted into reverie, then returned to the present. "Very well, Marianne shall see this Italian fellow. Perhaps in the time it takes for him to get here, we will come up with a better solution than to hurl flying bombs at the Prussians."

"It shall be done, Your Majesty," Tarlenheim said, rising.

"Excellent," the king said, also rising. "Now I shall watch swans. Good day to you, gentlemen. Advise me of further developments."

All bowed as the king strode from the room.

CHAPTER 3

THE WOMAN WHO CAME TO DINNER

Ruggiero Zambelli smiled across the table at his pretty guest. "More polletti, Contessa?"

The Countess Marianne Theresa Desirée set down her fork and pushed back from the table. "I can't eat another mouthful."

Signora Zambelli, seated next to her husband, shook her head disapprovingly. "*Contessa*, you're young, you're beautiful—such a pretty face—doesn't she have a pretty face, Ruggi?—but, my dear, you're too thin. You eat like a sparrow." She was a heavy woman with two chins, and rolls of fat everywhere. For all that, Marianne could see good features beneath the pink, puffy skin of her face.

La Signora whacked her youngest son's wrist with a spoon. "Little monkey! Where are your table manners?"

"Ouch!"

His six brothers all guffawed. Little Enrico rubbed his hand and scowled at his mother.

"What's the matter, *Contessa*," Ruggiero Zambelli said, "you don't like game hen?"

"I love game hen, but I've eaten three of them. And all the rest of the food . . ."

Mon Dieu, what a meal! It had started with endive, egg-drop, and cheese soup; followed by a pasta course, *spaghetti all' aglio, olio e peperoncini*; followed by fish, *triglie alla Livornese*, mullet Livorno style; followed by the game hen with chili peppers, served with new potatoes; *baggiane*, broad beans Umbrian style; and *funghi e zucchini alla Nepitella*, mushrooms and zucchini with mint.

And that wasn't counting the appetizers: Jerusalem artichokes with onion, deep-fried zucchini and mushrooms, celery, three kinds of olives, marinated fresh anchovies, and seven kinds of cheese. Still to come were salad and dessert. Marianne didn't know where she'd find room for the salad, let alone that enormous, scrumptious-looking apricot tart, *crostata d' albicocche*, sitting on the sideboard, flanked by bottles of dessert wine.

The wines. She must have drunk a barrel by now, and here was signore Zambelli offering her more.

Ruggiero Zambelli, president and chairman of the board of Zambelli Pyrotechnics of Florence, had a round face with a bulbous nose that protruded over a neat black mustache. His skin was a little on the swarthy side, set off by a bright sparkle to his eyes. Zambelli seemed perennially jolly. He had told many jokes and stories over the elaborate dinner.

There was enthusiasm and vigor in his manner. He was a man of passionate beliefs and convictions, although, as Marianne was finding out, some of those beliefs were a trifle . . . well, unconventional. At the moment, he was just engaging in polite dinner conversation. In his beautifully cut black formal dinner jacket and boiled shirt with emerald studs and cuff links, he was the suavest of hosts.

"You must try this," he said, speaking in German for her benefit. He knew no French. "It is a wine from Montefiascone, on the lake of Bolsena. The wine is called *Est*, with an *. . .* how you call it, an exclamation mark after it. *Est!*"

"Est!?"

"Yes. Latin. It means, 'Here it is.' You see, sometime back in the middle ages, this German bishop was traveling to Rome to see the Pope. And all along the way he send his servant to find the best wine for him. The servant, he mark the door of a good tavern with the word '*Est.*' That means, this tavern serves the best wine. Now, when the servant reach Montefiascone, which is not far from Rome, he find a wine he like so much, he write on the door '*Est! Est!! Est!!!*' With one, two, three exclamation mark. And that's what they name the wine after."

Zambelli poured Marianne a glass of straw-colored wine. She sipped. "Wonderful!"

"You like? Is good, no?"

"I love it. I think I am going to explode."

"She eats like a sparrow," La Signora told her husband.

Marianne belched. "Oh, *Pardonnez-moi.*"

Everyone laughed.

"You know, *Contessa*, that is the first time I see a lady of the nobility do the burp. Most of those ladies, you know, they would rather die than do that at the table."

"I have been known to do worse things," Marianne said.

Signora Zambelli eyed her dubiously. Marianne wasn't at all sure that La Signora entirely approved of her. Imagine, a woman in a man's profession. A woman soldier!

"I hope you have enjoyed the food, *Contessa*," the Signora said.

As disapproving as she might be, as a woman of the high bourgeoisie—her husband was a rich man—signora Zambelli was still awed by the nobility.

"It was absolutely . . ." Marianne's Italian was not at all good. "*Delizioso!*" She wanted to say heavenly, but couldn't remember the word. "Who is your cook?"

"Berenice is her name," signora Zambelli said. "She is with the family for years."

"*Straordinario.*"

"Your Italian is wonderful," signore Zambelli said. "I'm so glad there won't be problems when we speak to each other, while we work together on the rocket project."

Hmmm. *Signora* Zambelli wasn't jumping for joy over that, either.

Marianne was glad she didn't have to coax Zambelli into coming to Bavaria to see Ludwig. The moment she broached the subject, he accepted enthusiastically, to Marianne's immense relief. What she knew about rockets wouldn't stuff a flea. Then again, who knew anything about them but men like signore Zambelli and maybe Jules Verne, the insane Frenchman with all the outlandish ideas.

"How long will it take to transport your rocket vessel to Bavaria, signore?"

"Is a rocket *ship*, Mademoiselle. First, I gotta take apart. Then, she can be shipped."

"Oh, I see. Is it quite large?"

"She's measure eight meters from the tip to the tail."

"Is that big for a . . . rocket ship?"

Zambelli shook his head. "Dunno! No one is ever built the rocket ship before. She's the first. Would you like to see?"

"Certainly. Do you keep it near here?"

"No, not near the house. She's in a big shed on the edge of the property. I take you there."

"How long do you think it will take to ship the components of your rocket?" Marianne asked.

"Maybe two, three weeks. Some pieces, they very heavy. Big casings," he said, holding out his arms, "like this, big around. And the engine, she's very, very heavy. By wagon, she takes time up those mountain roads in the Alps."

"Couldn't you fly your ship to Bavaria?"

Zambelli's rich laughter made her smile. "I would love to. But the rocket, she's not ready to fly. Anyway, the neighbors, they don't like me shooting off rockets. They complain. No room, anyway. But in Bavaria. Ah, now that's different. You have mountains. Nobody live on them. I'm look on the map, and I see a . . . *come si dice* . . . high place, flat, over the Königsee."

"Plateau."

"Yes. And a big, big mountain near."

"The Zugspitze. It's the highest peak in Bavaria."

"If you shoot off a rocket from the plateau, she go on a trajectory, right over the Zugspitze."

"But that would take it into Austria."

"Ah. But you gotta talk to them. Get permission."

To Marianne's skeptical mind, this was exactly the fatal flaw in any plan to mount a Bavarian rocket project. There was no room in Bavaria to shoot off rockets. The country was landlocked except for its minuscule coast, which was just an oversized inlet of the North Sea. No matter where you shot the infernal thing, you'd hit somebody else's country. Or you'd hit your own.

Anyway, when Zambelli talked about his dreams, she heard a strong hint that he wasn't planning to shoot over any mountain. He was aiming at the moon, of all the crazy things to do! He had begun babbling about it as soon as Marianne told him of the king's desire to finance his rocket building.

Fly to the moon? Absurd notion.

The Zambelli estate in the Tuscan countryside was not far from Florence, in a rolling patchwork of field and garden, orchard and vineyard. Huge Romanesque villas bestrode the crests of the hills, well away from any bustling city.

The whole family came along on the short trip to the edge of the Zambelli holdings, all riding in a big, four-wheeled farm wagon. The boys sat in the wagon. *Signora* Zambelli sat on the seat between Marianne and her husband, who drove. Two lumbering dray horses pulled the wagon easily at a slow walk.

A large stone building lay ahead.

"Used to be the winery," Zambelli said. "My grandfather got out of the wine business. Lose too much money. But the grapes, they still there." He pointed to an unkempt vineyard off to the left.

Marianne's attention was on the building. "The rocket ship is inside?"

"That's right. I build it here, in my spare time. I would do it at the factory, but a fireworks factory has many small buildings, no big ones."

"Why is that?"

"So if one blow up, the whole works no go up with it."

"Oh."

Marianne suddenly realized that fireworks manufacturing was risky business. "Are there many accidents?"

Zambelli nodded dolefully. "My grandfather, he die in an explosion when he was seventy-one years old. One uncle die with him—he was inside the building. Fourteen years later, my brother, Rufino, he blow up, and three workers."

"*Mon Dieu!*"

Zambelli sighed. "He was only twenty-four years old. Bad, this business. Dangerous."

"*C'est dommage. Che peccato.*"

"Come inside," Zambelli said as he climbed down from the wagon. "I show you *La Bomba Grossa*."

"The Big Bomb?"

"Yes. I build the model of this, a little one. I set it off. She go up, then she blow up, *ba-boom!* So, I call the big one *La Bomba Grossa*. Come. Aida, stay here with the children."

"Aw, Papa, we want to come in!"

Signora Zambelli snapped, "You've seen the silly thing a thousand times! Let the lady see it in peace. Stay here. Luigino! Get back in the wagon, or you get a smack."

Marianne wondered if she had decoded Tom's telegraph message properly. Did he really want to bring this obviously eccentric back yard inventor to Bavaria to manufacture military ordnance? Warily, she approached the entrance, two huge pine barn doors with rusted cast-iron hinges.

Zambelli applied a key to a padlock on a chain, undid the chain, and pulled the right door open a little. He ushered Marianne into a vast interior that had obviously been augmented by the judicious tearing down of non-load-bearing walls. The greater part of the straw-covered floor was taken up by an immense craft with a shape like that of a sleek fish. Rakish fins sprouted dorsally and ventrally from both its middle and tail. Made of riveted sheet brass, the ship gleamed radiantly golden. A line of circular quartz windows, as on a sea vessel, ran along its side. A curved arrangement of windows adorned the base of a hump at the prow.

"So this is a rocket ship," Marianne said. "Are you sure you can make it blow up when it reaches the target?"

"*Mi scusi, Contessa?*"

"You know, blow up. The thing you shoot it at. Isn't the bomb supposed to blow up and destroy it?"

"Oh, no, *Contessa*. No. The rocket ship is not supposed to blow up. The model blow up by accident."

"Then you drop bombs from the ship?"

"No."

"Oh. But . . . what good is it?"

"What good? Mademoiselle, this ship will take me to the moon. To Mars! To all the planets. It is a spaceship."

Marianne nodded elaborately, feigning an understanding she did not have. "Ohhhhhh. A *space* ship."

"*Assolutamente.*"

"But I thought . . ." Marianne broke off, wondering if she had misread Tom's whole message.

"But, signore Zambelli," she tried again. "I was under the impression your ship was meant for war."

"War! *Madonna,* no! This spaceship is for humanity to go to the stars! It is not for to kill people."

Completely confused, Marianne stammered, "Well . . . I'm not sure . . ."

"Let me ask you, *Contessa* does your King Ludwig want me to build bombs for war?" Zambelli made a sweeping motion with his hand, his face adamant. "I will not do it."

"I see." Marianne shrugged. "I must communicate with my superiors before I can continue negotiations. If there are any to continue at all."

As she walked with Zambelli around the ship, Marianne noticed for the first time that she was a little taller than he. Zambelli was deep in thought.

"I do not understand," he said slowly. "I know of your King Ludwig. I think I know his soul, and he does not seem a man who likes to make war. I thought he had heard about my project . . . maybe he read my book . . . I write a small book. I'm hoping, dreaming about a great, rich man who would give me the money to finish my spaceship. It needs much work, this ship. The engine, she no run good. She needs work. I can't put my money in it."

"Why?"

"Aida, my wife. She forbid me to spend any more money." Zambelli shrugged, then chuckled impishly. "And my other brothers, who own the company with me. They think I'm crazy. Aida, she kill me if she know how much I already spend. But that's my secret. Anyway, I think I know your king. He is not a man of war. He is a poet. He love opera. Sure, Wagner, but it's still opera. Almost. How can a man like that want to kill people? No, I think . . . I think maybe he read my book. It's a story about men who go to the moon. Now maybe, they go in this. My ship. To the moon."

Zambelli stopped abruptly.

"I go with you, *Contessa*," he exclaimed. "I go with you to see your King Ludwig. I must talk with him. I must know if his soul is different from what I think. I will see if he wants to make war or go to the stars."

Marianne smiled. That was one way to achieve her mission objective. Let the rocket experts argue it out! "Wonderful. Can you leave tomorrow morning?"

CHAPTER 4

RHYME ANSWERS THE CALL

Rhyme's workshop did not occupy the bottom-most level of Castle Falkenstein. Although no one could say for sure, rumor warned of drear, dank dungeons on the level beneath the workshop; the oubliette, reserved for the foulest traitors to the crown. However, none of the castle's dungeons had seen much use.

The combined workshop and lab was drear enough, made mysterious by racks of bubbling chemical apparatus, retorts and such (this experiment had been running for a full year, and Rhyme would tell no one what it was about), giant spark coils, banks of curious instruments, and rows of benches busy with general mechanical clutter. Dwarf clutter. The place struck most people as typically dwarfen. A penchant for the mechanical marked dwarfs, and that went double for the arcanely mechanical. Heaps of greasy gears lay piled here and there. In other places gears, shafts, and universal joints were linked together into quirky assemblages designed for obscure mechanical purposes.

One such object, a melon-sized spherical contraption, lay on the bench in front of Rhyme. Using a long screwdriver, he teased a tiny screw inside the open latticework of the thing. The contraption resembled an orrery, a small planetarium, one depicting ancient Ptolemaic astronomy. Its works suggested the whirring of epicycles, but this was no planetarium.

Rhyme grunted, trying to get the tiny screw to turn.

"Damn the thing," he said finally, and gave up. Withdrawing the delicate screwdriver, he set it aside.

"Rhyme?"

"Eh?"

Rhyme looked around, but saw no one. He shook his head.

"Rhyme Enginemaster."

"What?" he asked irritably. Another glance about the place showed that he was alone. He got off his stool and went to the foot of the stone stairs that led to the entrance door. The door was shut and the stairs were empty.

Rhyme scratched his head. "Damnedest thing."

He went back to the bench and tinkered some more. Then he got up again and went farther down the bench to yet another curious contraption, a brass box about as big as a large jewelry case; perhaps a little larger. The open top exposed the works: an intricate brass clockwork mechanism of tiny gears, wheels, screws, linkages, and more linkages. A device that looked something like an antique typewriter fronted the affair.

Rhyme hit a few of the keys, which were inscribed with arcane symbols. Pins rose from within the typewriter, perforating a length of paper tape. Rhyme hit a few more keys, then turned a small crank on the side of the box. The punched paper tape slid into the works.

Rhyme turned a larger crank to stoke up energy in the clockwork mechanism. He then hit a button, and the brass innards of the analytical engine began to crank and turn and spin, making a metallic chattering noise.

While this went on, Rhyme brooded over the mechanism. Abruptly, the chattering ceased. Paper tape inched from the side of the brass box.

When the output finished, Rhyme ripped off the length of tape and held it up to a nearby candle. He scanned the position of the neatly punched holes.

"Hmmmph," he said.

"Rhyme Enginemaster," came the voice again.

"Blast it, who calls?" Rhyme looked about wildly.

"Here, Rhyme. In the mirror."

"What mirror?" he shouted.

The voice had been muffled and barely audible. Yet it was familiar.

"Answer me!" Rhyme yelled. "Where in the name of all that's unholy are you?"

"In the mirror. The mirror I sent you."

"*What* bloody mirror?"

"I can't see you, so it must be covered."

"Of all the ridiculous . . ."

Rhyme left the bench and walked in circles. "Mirror. Mirror . . . where in blazes . . . ?"

Stopping abruptly, he turned to a pile of heterogeneous junk in a corner. He threw aside boxes, crates, coils of wire, wood frames, and other oddments before revealing a flat rectangular package wrapped in brown paper and tied with string. The package had arrived months ago, but he had never got a round to opening it. Whipping out his pocketknife, he cut the wrapping away, revealing an old looking glass.

"Ah!"

It was an ancient mirror, of a good size for an antique, but the glass was dark and murky, and the frame, plain wood. In its day, long ago, it had doubtless adorned the dressing table of a fine lady.

Rhyme picked it up and blew off some dust before fetching it to a workbench, where he stood it behind a small toolbox and up against the wall. After sorting through a pile of rags and coming up with a relatively clean one, he gave the glass a quick wipe. Satisfied, he stepped back and peered into the mirror's depths.

Dimly, he saw his own reflection.

"What gives?" he asked impatiently.

Suddenly, he saw a second image superimposed over his own. Another dwarf, dressed in a morning coat and stovepipe hat, peered out at him.

"Who the devil are you?" Rhyme demanded.

"You don't recognize your cousin?"

"Cousin? What cousin?"

"Alberich. Alberich Ringmaker."

"Who?" Suddenly, recognition dawned. "Oh. Yes, I remember you. Haven't seen you in ages."

Alberich grunted. "Well, don't fall all over yourself with gladness." Abruptly his manner changed; he forced a smile and affected a conciliatory tone. "Yes, it has been a long spell, hasn't it? Congratulations on your new name, Enginemaster. Fine name, noble name."

"It'll do. What's on your mind? And what's this business, anyway? You sent me this mirror. Why?"

"As a gift, Rhyme, from cousin to cousin. It's an ancient magical artifact. A Sending Glass. It captures an image much like a camera obscura and transmits it a great distance. The image can then be picked up with any old mirror, depending on where you direct the sending."

"If the magic mirror's here, how are you sending?"

"I'm using another magic glass, a twin to yours, probably created by the same wizard, long ago. The beauty of these, though, is that the receiving mirror need not be magic."

"So you said." Rhyme squinted and tilted his head. "The damned thing's no good. Your image is hazy and indistinct."

Alberich waved a hand. "That's nothing. This one puts out a little extraneous smoke while operating. I sent you the better of the two."

"So, it's done with smoke and mirrors, eh? But enough of this, tell me what you want."

"To tell the truth, cousin, I had no reason to hail you other than to send cousinly greetings and wish you well. And of course, to test the device."

"Well, it works, to an extent. And I have to admit it's a clever trick. I'll have to experiment with the idea, see if I can combine it with my engines."

"Why bother with infernal engines when you have this mirror, gratis?"

"*Gratis?*" Rhyme snorted. "You must think me a bigger fool than you are, Alberich."

If Alberich took affront, he concealed it with an oily smile. "Not at all. You are young, but very clever in your own right. Especially when it comes to sorcerous engines."

"I have a certain talent, I suppose. But what is it you want from me in trade for the mirror trick?"

"A Babbage engine."

"Nothing sorcerous about a Babbage engine," Rhyme said.

"I did not say that sorcery was needed, especially, except perhaps in small doses to solve some physical problems. I want to know if you can reduce the weight of a Babbage engine to something on the order of a three-week-old shoat."

Rhyme's eyes darted to the analytical engine on the bench nearby. "Doesn't sound impossible. Why do you ask?"

Alberich shrugged. "That's what I want. A calculating engine of extremely reduced size and weight. The weight factor is the most critical."

"I see. And in return I'd get to keep the mirror?" Rhyme scowled. "Try again."

"Can we make a deal? Name your price."

"I'll have to think about it. Where can I reach you?"

"I've taken a job in Prussia."

"Well, hell's ballocks, you've lived in Prussia all your life."

"Yes. But I've taken a job—in fact my entire dwarfhold has taken a job—with the government."

"Working for Bismarck, are we?"

Alberich shrugged. "One has to make a living somehow. Are you implying that one human is better than another?"

Rhyme scuffed his left boot against the stones. "They're all alike, you know that. Big, dumb, and nasty."

"Exactly. So what do you care who I'm working for? I want the engine. We need it here for our job."

"What is your job?"

"Can't talk about that."

"Oh, fiddle."

Alberich's image leaned forward a bit. He peered from the murky mirror depths. "This is Falkenstein, is it not? Nice place."

Rhyme moved to one side, trying to block a view of the far workbench. "They treat me right here. I'm never short of beer and sausage."

"I can't see much, unfortunately, but it looks like a fine setup as a workshop." Alberich straightened. "Well, can we make a deal?"

"I don't know about the mirror thing. What practical value would it have?"

"As a communication device? Are you joking? Look, I have something to trade, and I think it's a good thing I'm offering. What I want in return is something that is well within your power to grant. Unless, of course, your reputation is . . how shall we say, inflated?"

Rhyme's eyes flashed green fire. "Inflate your tally-whacker, you toad, and then stick it up—"

Alberich held up a placating hand. "Peace. I mean you no insult.

"Well, you could have fooled me. Here's your answer. Take back your mirror and I'll keep my Babbage."

Alberich held up a hand. "No, no, keep it. You are under no obligation."

"You've got that right." Rhyme cocked a thumb. "Get out of my looking glass, cousin."

Alberich leaned to the left as if reaching for something. "As you wish. Be warned, though. Rude treatment of a kinsman is not taken lightly in this dwarfhold. We will repay, with interest."

"Repay it any damned way you like, Fancy-Clothes. Good-bye."

Alberich's image wavered and grew dim. Presently, it faded.

"Damnedest nonsense," Rhyme complained. "Wonder what the devil he wanted with my benchtop analytical? Well, no matter. Never trusted the bastard, anyway."

He started to turn away, then considered the mirror again, scratching his beard. "Hmm, I wonder."

Taking the mirror, he carried it to the benchtop analytical and stood it behind the device.

"Now, if I adapted it a bit, I wonder if I could project the data on the tape to show in the glass? Hmmmm. Might work."

Reseating himself on the stool, Rhyme commenced to think.

CHAPTER 5

THE ITALIAN GAMBIT

King Ludwig glanced around the conference table at his ministers and advisors "Tell me again, why should I see this Italian gentleman, this signore . . . ?"

"Zambelli," Tarlenheim supplied. "Ruggiero Zambelli."

"Yes, signore Zambelli. You say he's a . . . he makes fireworks?"

"Yes," Olam said. "He's the closest thing to an aerospace . . . er, I mean a rocket scientist that we can come up with. He's no ordinary Italian fireworks maker. With the special interest and enthusiasm he has for rocketry, you could say he's von Bremen's Italian counterpart."

"I see," the king said, with distaste. "And he knows how to construct these diabolical rocket machines?"

"He has plans aplenty," Colonel Tarlenheim said. "If what Olam says is true, some of them are . . . how shall I put it? Eccentric, to say the least."

"Visionary," Olam said. "He vanity-published a sort of novel, call it a scientific romance, on rocketry and the possibility of space travel. I found it truly remarkable. He apes Jules Verne, but he's something of a Jules Verne character, himself."

The king nodded, his curiosity slightly piqued. "I see. Space travel. By which you mean . . . ?"

"Travel to outer space, Your Majesty," Olam said. "Beyond the atmosphere . . . to the moon and other planets, possibly."

"Indeed," the king said. "Travel to the moon. What a fantastic notion."

"It's well within the realm of the theoretically feasible," Olam said.

"And what a romantic notion, in a way," the king added. "I wonder what it's made of."

Olam said, "The moon? Rock, mostly. Uh, so astronomers suspect."

"Really?" Ludwig said with some disappointment. "Rock. How mundane. I was thinking . . . something more rarefied. More ethereal, less earthly."

"It's not green cheese," Olam said with a smile.

"Green cheese?"

"I think," the colonel said, "we'd best stick to earthly matters. I care nothing about travel to the moon. My concern is for the security of the realm."

"Well," the king said, "security is, of course, always paramount in my mind. But there are aspects of this business that do intrigue me, much to my surprise. You say this Italian fellow is waiting to see me?"

"May I bring him in now, Your Majesty?" Pfistermeister asked, rising.

"Please do, Herr Pfistermeister."

"I shall, sire."

The cabinet secretary stepped past the white-lacquered doors. He returned very shortly with Ruggiero Zambelli, nattily dressed in a black morning jacket, maroon bow tie with matching patterned silk waistcoat, and gray striped trousers. The Italian cut was tastefully stylish.

"Your Majesty," Pfistermeister said, "may I present signore Ruggiero Zambelli."

The king said, "*piacere*, Signore. You have our leave to sit with us."

Zambelli bowed deeply. "Your Majesty, a great honor. A great honor indeed." To Ludwig, his German was thickly-accented but comprehensible. "I have heard so much about the great king of Bavaria, what a great and noble heart, so generous a *padrone* of the artist . . . this is wonderful, I . . . I—"

The Italian seemed almost overcome.

"Tut, tut, do sit down, Signore."

Zambelli looked around uncertainly. "It is permitted to sit in the presence of the king?"

"I insist, Signore. We tend to be informal in this room. Please seat yourself here, next to me."

"Thank you, thank you. His Majesty is too kind."

"So, signore Zambelli," Ludwig began. "Tell me of your plans in the field of rocket machines. Keep to general terms, please. I have not the mind for technical *mimetia* as do these other gentlemen."

"Yes, Your Majesty. It will be my honor. I have a plan, Your Majesty. I plan a feat that will make the world shout praises for the great king of Bavaria. It will astound humanity!"

"Fascinating," the king said mildly. "I can't wait to hear it."

Colonel Tarlenheim leaned forward to ask pointedly, " signore Zambelli, can you construct a rocket missile that will reach Berlin?"

Zambelli laughed. "Berlin? That is a walk down the street. I can . . . Your Majesty, I can build a rocket airship that could fly you to New York City in one hour."

Ludwig smiled. "I'm afraid I have no plans to go to New York City in the near future. However, if I did undertake such a trip, doubtless I would be pleased to board your rocket airship."

"Thank you, Your Majesty. And so would the world. People would pay any amount of money for a ticket on such an airship! Think of the money that could be made just in delivering the mail!"

Zambelli gestured wildly. "Imagine delivery to another continent overnight! You could have a company that did nothing but this thing. An air express company! Delivering special packages, important documents. The diplomats would welcome it! There is no telling . . ."

"Signore, Signore," the king said, placing a royal hand on Zambelli's sleeve. "Please, your enthusiasm is infectious, but try to contain yourself."

"A thousand apologies, Your Gracious Majesty." Zambelli took out a paisley print handkerchief and began to mop his brow. "But I do not lie. The possibilities are endless. And that is only part of the thing I have to tell you. The grandest is what I will do with the big rocket."

"Uh, the big rocket?"

"Yes, *La Bomba Grossa*, the rocket that I will take to the moon!"

Pfistermeister and the colonel could not suppress a guffaw.

Zambelli glowered at them. "Ah, I see you great gentlemen think I am funny. I assure you, sirs, I no joke. I can do this thing, if I can solve only one problem."

His expression saddened. "The rocket have the power, you see, but not the control. All at once, she go off, like the fireworks. *Ba-boom!* Something is needed to control the burning, you understand? Also, I need money. Not much, because I put my own money already. I nearly drive myself bankrupt! A little more money, and . . . *whoooosh! La Grossa*, she fly. And I fly her to the moon!"

The king glanced around the table, his eyes finally settling on the wizard. "Morrolan. You've been very quiet. What do you think of this? Is it possible?"

The wizard said, "Not without sorcery, my king."

"No sorcery!" Zambelli exclaimed. "I can do it without the devil!"

Morrolan laughed. "I should think it some help if your rocket propellant were ensorceled to burn longer and more forcefully."

Tom Olam put in, "We also might adapt the Heat Engine for rocket use. It's a possibility, anyway, maybe for the upper stages."

Zambelli considered. "Perhaps, some sorcery. This might be. I don't deny that the problem is very big. But I can do it! I am sure!"

"And I'm sure the world will lavish you with laurel wreaths, Signore," the king assured him. "You will receive all the kudos you deserve."

"Ah, but the world is hard, practical," Zambelli complained. "They want to know, sure, you go to the moon, but what about the price of linguine? Practical! And I am practical, too. Otherwise, you don't make money in business. I have done good in business, but I have the poetry in me as well as the business. You understand, Your Majesty?"

"Oh, yes," the king said sincerely, nodding his head. "Yes, indeed. I, too, 'have the poetry' in me. More so than most men, I'd wager."

"Yes, that is why I come to you, Great King!"

"And you want to fly . . . to the moon. And New York City."

"Uh . . . yes, Your Majesty. I have a sister in New York. She's move there from Italy, get married. She has two little ones."

"Wonderful, wonderful." The king was lost in reverie. "You know, signore Zambelli . . ."

"Yes, Great King?"

"I rather like this little project of yours. I do not like rockets in themselves. I find the thought of killing people repellent in the extreme."

"Killing people?" Zambelli looked around anxiously, then implored, "Great King, did I say anything of killing people? It is true, I sell the signal rockets to the army. To the Pope and his army, I sell them! I must make bread to live, to feed my children. I have seven children, Your Majesty, and they eat like the horse. Always, they eat, and their mamma feeds them more!

"But my rockets, not for killing. No, no! I make my rockets to take a man to the moon. I say it: a man will one day stand on the moon! And on Mars, and Venus. And then, Majesty. And then . . . out to the stars!"

"Wonderful, Signore. A great ambition," the king said dreamily. "A noble undertaking, indeed. To stand on the moon and look at the earth. That surely would change the heart of any man. To see the home of mankind and realize that all men are brothers!"

A beatific smile broke out on Zambelli's swarthy face. "*Assolutamente!* We understand each other . . . *perfetto! Perfettissimo!*"

The wizard Morrolan had been listening thoughtfully. "His Majesty makes a good point. We might not need to build rockets to hurl against the Prussians if we are able to convince them that we can, at any time, retaliate against their attack."

"Personally, I have my doubts about that," Tarlenheim warned. "Good intentions are no substitute for a sword when facing an armed foe."

"Perhaps," Morrolan said, "but recall, Colonel, that young Captain Olam has told us of just such a situation occurring on his own side of the Veil. 'Mutually Assured Deterrence,' I believe he called it."

"'Mutually Assured Destruction,' actually," Tom said.

"Heavens," Ludwig exclaimed. "What madness!"

"Kind of," Tom admitted, shrugging.

"Interesting," said Morrolan. "Nevertheless, you claim, do you not, that this policy held the peace between two great rival empires for forty years? And how many rocket weapons were there on each side?"

Tom began, "Well—"

"One will suffice for us," Tarlenheim said. "For now, at least. Then again, we have absolutely no assurance that such a thing can work."

"The Prussians have proved they can work," Tom said.

"I concede the point. Anyway, Morrolan, your plan might be feasible if we had a working rocket machine to show off. To frighten them a little."

Ludwig nodded. "I am in favor of this ploy. Then we are agreed? We shall build a single superior rocket and demonstrate to the Prussians that they will be ill-advised to challenge us."

Heads nodded around the table.

King Ludwig leaned toward Zambelli. "Signore, I will patronize your poetic undertaking. Take up the details with my ministers. I— Oh, dear."

Re nobile! Re nobile e gentile!

Zambelli had fairly fallen out of his chair to one knee and was smothering the king's left hand in kisses, zeroing in on the royal signet.

"Please, Signore," the king protested, withdrawing a damp hand. "It's not a holy relic."

Red-faced, Zambelli scrambled to his feet, while gales of laughter burst from those around the table.

CHAPTER 6

I COULD HAVE FENCED ALL NIGHT

Rococo splendor suffused the sumptous grand ballroom in Falkenstein. With all the chandeliers lighted, the gilt fairly blinded. Aurochs and cherubs crowded the pediments and friezes. Tracery crawled along the walls and up the pilasters, busied itself on the ceiling, and wriggled back down again, budding golden seashells along the way. The walls were rose with lemon trim, the parquetry golden-orange, the ceiling phosphorescent yellow stars and moons swimming in a dark blue sky. Color and finery showed everywhere, while the entire room took on a lambent glow from the warm amber light of a thousand candles.

Everyone in the resplendent crowd had dressed to the nines. It had been a good year locally for the debutante crop and many were in evidence for the Spring Cotillion. Despite the clutter of sweet young things, the ball was a full-tilt affair of state, with an admixture of Bayern's top social strata in attendance, including many foreign dignitaries, as well as the Prussian ambassador, his wife, and some of his aides.

Tom Olam stood near the refreshment table, drinking punch and gazing about. Lots of uniforms tonight—cavalry, hussars, lancers. The nineteenth century was great for military dress, he mused. He looked down at his own blue and gold cavalry outfit, remembering that he had meant to get it pressed. All the planning meetings had kept him from finding time.

He'd spent hours with the tech staff of the Secret Service debating the best way to overfly the Prussian rocket test range on the Baltic coast. A Bayernese aerowarship could stay well above the range of any naval gun, but the possibility that von Bremen and his engineers had already deployed one or two anti-air rocket batteries was unsettling. One direct hit on an aerowarship's huge gas nacelle would bring it down. What, then, to do?

Tom had been given the job of gathering all available information on rocketry and von Bremen's work in that field. It was the most challenging assignment yet in his not-overlong career as a secret service operative.

"Tom!"

Olam turned to see the Countess Marianne approaching. "Wow," he said to himself, stunned anew each time he saw her.

She wore one of her more elaborate silk ball gowns over wide hoops. Pink, draped in white and gold ribbons and bedecked in sham roses around the neckline and down the sides, the gown was as feminine as Marianne herself, for all that she was a crack shot, a diabolically lethal swords woman, and an expert on horseback. She was lovely besides, and tonight, with her hazel eyes starred by candle flame highlights and her chestnut-brown hair fringed with an amber aura, she was breathtaking.

Tom closed his jaw and smiled. "Italy agrees with you," he told her.

"You are the wallflower this evening," Marianne said. "Put down your drink and ask one of these lovely young women to dance."

"Dance with the debs?" Tom sighed. "I guess it's my duty."

"*Absolument, mon cher. The punch, c'est bon?*"

"Sweet," Tom said. "*Douce*. Like you."

She pinched his cheek. "You are the charming young officer tonight. Sweep one of these debs off her feet."

"I'd rather dance with you all night."

"Not proper. No more than two dances with the same partner. We danced already. People will talk."

"Let them talk," Tom said. "I'll make an honest woman of you. Everything on the up and up, I always say."

"No. Tongues will wag. I am now already the fallen woman, almost. Everything must be . . . how do you say . . . up yours."

"On the up and up," Tom corrected with a chuckle.

"Whatever." Marianne laughed with him. "Dance!"

"I can't just now." Tom lowered his voice. "Our secret agent in the Prussian embassy is supposed to make contact with me tonight. He has information on the rocket program. Or so his messages said."

"Oh, yes. The one called Goethe." After looking about, Marianne leaned over. "Who is he?"

A deeper view of the lovely agent's shadowed cleavage momentarily distracted Tom. He cleared his throat. "I have only a general description. Goethe's identity is strictly hush-hush. Tarlenheim has the file on him, but he wouldn't even let me see it. Said the less I knew, the better. Goethe's our top agent."

"Or double agent," Marianne suggested.

Tom nodded ruefully. "Over the years, it's been touch and go as to whose side he's on—but . . . his information is always impeccable."

"We should stop talking," Marianne said, sliding her gaze sideways. "The walls have ears."

"We should stop talking shop at a social function," Tom agreed.

"We should stop working at a social function," Marianne said, playfully tapping his arm.

"We should, but the Secret Service never rests."

As the orchestra struck up another number, Marianne said, "And now, I should dance with the Austrian ambassador. Have a good time."

Tom watched her glide away. She had a habit of suddenly saying good-bye and disappearing. It wasn't rude so much as businesslike. Tom had never minded, but tonight he brooded a little. He wished she had stuck around a bit longer. He was getting an antsy feeling about the evening.

The orchestra oom-pahed away, and Tom sighed, growing impatient. How long would he have to wait for the agent to make contact?

A voice came from behind him. "Splendid evening."

"Eh?" Tom spun around. His gaze fell on a distinguished gentleman in a tuxedo, who stood gazing out onto the dance floor.

"Ah, yes," Tom said. "Splendid evening. Uh . . . sir."

The man's eyes did not meet Tom's. "You're not dancing, young man. A spring night is especially good for dancing. To dance, to love."

"Spring," Tom said. "Great time. Flowers bloom. Roses bud."

"Ah, roses," said the man, still not meeting Tom's gaze. "'*Sah ein Knab ein Röslein stehn, Roslein auf der Heiden . . .*'"

"'*War so jung und morgenschön,*'" Tom replied, "'*Lief er schnell, es nah zu sehn, sah's mit vielen Freuden.*'" "Goethe, I believe," he added.

"Pleased to meet you," the agent said.

"What do you have for me?"

The man spoke casually, his eyes curiously diverted, as if addressing an invisible person on Tom's left. "Meet me in the garden in five minutes, near the big elm tree. Is there a young lady whom you can trust?"

"Yes."

"Bring her. It would look best to escort a lady love into the garden. Be sure you are not followed."

"Will do," Tom said, and watched the man sidle off toward the big French windows along the far wall. The windows—doors really—led out to a piazza with steps leading down to the south end of the castle's extensive formal garden.

Tom made a circuit of the dance floor, looking for Marianne and hoping she wasn't dancing. He did not relish cutting in on a dignitary. He was thankful to see her standing under one of the big chandeliers, talking with a group of people.

He stepped up to her. "There you are, Countess."

She turned to him and smiled slyly. "Still wilting along the wall, Captain Olam?"

"Maybe I need watering, or, better yet, a breath of fresh air. Would you care to accompany me on a stroll in the garden?" Tom extended his arm, his eyes adding extra emphasis.

She understood immediately. "I'd be delighted," she said, and excused herself. She and Tom moved in a leisurely manner toward the French windows.

Paper lanterns placed at intervals partially lighted the garden below. A few couples strolled the darker moonlit paths. Tom was aware of Marianne's subtle perfume, but romance was for other couples tonight.

He fervently wished that he had asked how to identify an elm tree. He had seen elm trees, surely, but wasn't sure that he could pick one out in the dark might have chosen a more obvious meeting place.

They soon discovered there were no trees in the garden, itself, but many lining the borders. Few deserved the appellation "big." The tallest by far was a poplar, and those skinny trees, Tom could indeed identify in the dark. A single large deciduous tree stood off to the right.

Tom and Marianne made their way down the stone steps to the maze of stone pathways that threaded through compulsively neat hedgerows. After following a row of primroses, they turned right, making for the garden's edge, then took a few more turns, always keeping the giant elm in sight.

A thought asserted itself at the back of Tom's mind: if Castle Falkenstein had been magicked together not very long ago, how did the elm get so big? He decided the answer was implicit in the question.

They spotted the agent sitting on a bench across from the elm tree, quietly smoking a cigar.

"Good evening," Goethe said, rising. "I do not wish to be rude, Mademoiselle, but I have important business to discuss with this young man. We have no time for introductions."

"I quite understand," Marianne said. "I'll keep a lookout."

"Ah," Goethe said, looking at Tom with a twinkle in his eye, "a lady agent."

"One of the best."

"Sit down, please. Will you have a cigar?" Goethe proffered a beautiful gold case.

"Thanks, I don't smoke."

"Filthy habit, but I quite like it. The garden is for smokers, lest they bother the delicate nasal membranes of the ladies, so I have good reason to be out here."

Tom looked about before seating himself on the other end of the bench. "There's no one near, anyway."

"You are Captain Olam, then?"

"Right," Tom said.

"I have a report that says you were involved in the destruction of His Imperial Majesty's airship *Gottland*, one week ago."

"I happened to be passing by."

Goethe cracked a smile. "Very droll. Your reputation for grace under fire is well-founded, if the reports are accurate."

"We've been waiting for the other shoe to drop, diplomatically speaking."

"You won't hear a thing. My embassy is fully informed of the incident, but for obvious reasons the Prussian government does not want to draw attention to, shall we say, certain doings off the Baltic coast. The Swedes are already alarmed, though they won't breathe a word. Those rocket contraptions have been frightening Swedish fishermen to death."

"So they are rockets. Steam-powered rockets."

Goethe stared at Tom. "I thought you knew that, already."

"I did. Just checking."

"The Prussians would be extremely curious to discover how you knew they were rockets. The project is shrouded in the utmost secrecy. No one in the world should even know what a ballistic rocket missile is."

Tom just smiled.

Goethe grinned again. "Ah, but you are the man of mystery, are you not? From beyond the Faerie Veil. Who can guess what strange thoughts course through that vast and anachronistic mind?"

"I'm no Lamont Cranston, but I know what I know."

"Eh? I'm not familiar—" Goethe broke off, nodding sagely and puffing on the cigar. "I have heard that you are given to cryptic utterances."

"Sorry. What do you have for me?"

"Ah, my friend. My co-conspirator. My association with your organization has been a long and, for me, a lucrative one. If I had any technical information—plans, notebooks, graphs, drawings, anything, which of course is exactly what you want and need—I would hand them over to you with great pleasure, and with every expectation of great remuneration. But, alas, I have none to give. I work in an embassy, and engineering specifications are seldom found in diplomatic pouches."

"We weren't expecting that from you. Can you tell me if Rupert Hauptmann died in the crash of the *Gottland?*"

"My information is that all hands were lost. But I can tell you that Hauptmann is . . . rather, was . . . heading up the entire rocket research project."

"Really. He must have been promoted."

"Indeed he was. He is now a colonel, I believe. Have you ever heard of Karl Friedrich von Bremen?"

"Yes."

"He died not long ago. Hauptmann has commandeered his entire estate near Peenemunde, on the Baltic, for use as a research facility."

Again, for Tom, the name reverberated. "No doubt security is very tight."

"The tightest. The project has been veritably shrouded in secrecy."

"They've done a good job. The rocket took us totally by surprise. We were on a routine patrol of the Prussian coast when we spotted the test flight."

"The entire project is rather anomalous, isn't it?" Goethe said. "I suspect a supernatural impetus."

"It has the smell of Unseelie," Tom agreed. "That's for sure."

"Well, good luck in trying to cope with it," Goethe said.

"You can't give us anything useful, at all?"

"I didn't say that. Do you know that von Bremen published some of his work?"

"We've had the Royal Librarian trolling for a copy of his book."

"You mean *The Rocket in Military History*? That was written for the general public. Sold very few copies. It doesn't contain much that you don't already know. I was referring to his technical treatise. He published it in three volumes, on his own, privately printed. Few copies made their way into bookstores. Very rare items, very rare indeed. Prussian agents have been scouring the continent and buying up all existing copies."

"I guess we're a little late. Do you have an idea where we could get hold of this treatise? More to the point, do you know what's in it?"

"I'm not sure that any remain out of Prussian hands. A stray copy may exist in a private library. I can give you the name of a bookstore in Paris that might have a set, or up until recently might have had one. The store was mentioned in a secret dispatch to the Prussian embassy in Paris, and I have a feeling it relates to this matter. The name of the bookstore is Giroud, in Montparnasse. As to what's in the treatise, it's everything you need. Detailed engineering data, results of experiments, tests, design drawings, and so forth."

"When did that dispatch go through?"

"About three days ago. There still may be time to secure a copy, if you can get an agent to Giroud quickly enough. You do have an agent in Paris, by the way?" Goethe plucked the cigar from his lips and chuckled. "But of course you won't tell me, and you shouldn't."

Tom only grinned. "Nice evening, isn't it?"

"Splendid. Sorry I don't have more information. The only other lead I can give you is that certain British industrial barons might be involved in the Prussian project."

"Any idea who?"

"Gordon-Smythe, for one."

"Wellington Steel and Fabrication. Makes sense. Advanced metallurgy, new materials."

"Lord Montague, for another."

"Steam engines. Of course."

"And Ashburton Parkes."

"Chemicals," Tom said. "I wonder if they're already think-ing of the next step."

"I beg your pardon?"

"The next developmental step in rocketry. Steam is a pretty inefficient way to run a rocket engine. I'm guess-ing they're looking forward to solid-fuel technology. Maybe liquid-fuel."

Goethe said, "You'll forgive my lack of acquaintance with these technical matters."

"What's important is that Bismarck is still actively forging an alliance with the British Steam Lords."

"Oh, my, yes. For him it's a perfect marriage. Prussian militarism and British engineering. How better to rule the world? Or at least to dominate New Europa."

"Meanwhile, the Unseelie sit behind the curtains, pulling the strings."

"That, too, my friend."

"Anything else, Goethe?"

The secret agent smiled wistfully. "I should be used to

being called that by now, but it always strikes a sad note in me. I'm something of a poet manqué, you know."

"I didn't know. I've dabbled myself, some."

"What sensitive German youth hasn't fancied himself a poet after the model of Goethe? '*Röslein, Röslein, Röslein rot, Röslein auf der—* ' *HerrGott!*"

The haft of a dagger suddenly materialized in Goethe's chest, as if springing full-blown from it.

Tom reached vainly for him, but Goethe toppled over, rolled off the bench, and fell to the stone pathway.

From his left, Tom saw a blur of pink. He heard the rustle of petticoats. Marianne was running for the bushes surrounding the elm.

"I saw him!" she yelled before plunging through a curtain of foliage.

Tom drew his sword and followed. The thick bramble of bushes continued down the slope. Tom forced his way through thorns, heedless of sharp needle points snagging him and stinging his face and hands.

"He's gone," he heard Marianne say. "Down the hill. Disappeared."

When Tom caught up to her, he saw she had a sword in her hand. He laughed. "Where were you keeping that thing?"

A half smile tilted her lips. "What good is a hooped gown if you can't hide a sword under it?"

"Ingenious." Tom took her arm. "We'd better get back to the elm. Goethe bought it, I think."

"He bought something?"

"No, I mean he's dead. It was so quick, I'm wondering . . ."

A voice, inhuman and rasping, came out of the darkness. "Mortals, prepare to die."

"*Sacre bleu!*" Marianne said with a gasp.

Tom said evenly, "I do believe there's Faerie about."

"Indeed, mortal."

Two creatures sprang from the bushes. They were Faerie, all right, of the Unseelie Court, the most unsavory stripe of Faerie. Their particular species or classification was hard to pin down, as most forms of Faerie creature could change shape at will. These looked to be general utility goblins, wielding Faerie-silver swords. They were primarily humanoid, with spiked tails, wicked claws, and huge reptilian taloned feet. In "reality" (whatever that meant when speaking of Faerie) they may have been human-looking Faerie to begin with, or perhaps phookas or other shapechangers.

Tom had fallen afoul of Unseelie before. He knew that he and Marianne were in mortal danger. The best thing was to make a break for it. They weren't far from the garden. He could still hear the music from the ballroom.

But the demons moved fast, too fast, their strong legs thrashing the shrubbery aside as they broke from cover. Running was no solution.

"Only two of you?" Tom asked with as much sang-froid as he could muster.

"More can join us, mortal, in the twinkling of an eye."

One of the creatures promptly split into two smaller versions of itself.

"You could reach a point of diminishing returns doing that," Tom said. To Marianne, he added, "I'll take the pair."

"*Oui, mon cher.* But first—" Marianne pulled a ribbon at her waist, causing a ripping sound. The skirt collapsed and fell away. Stepping from the folds of silk and crinoline, she stood unashamedly bare-legged, wearing just a garter belt.

"Wow, that's slick," Tom said, trying not to stare. "Rig that yourself?"

"Of course."

Tom swung about as the demons charged. The thicket rang with the clash of steel against Faerie silver. Tom needed all his skills as he parried and thrust with his two opponents. He lost sight of Marianne, but the clang of her sword against that of her unearthly opponent continued at his back.

Tom hacked and slashed, fended off one assailant, whirled and jabbed at the other, then beat a retreat behind a large forsythia bush. He ducked behind a tree, got his bearings, then charged out, attacking with a lunge and a slash and managing to nick the pointed ear of one of the creatures.

The other jumped from behind the bush and nearly decapitated him. Tom ducked, then sent the blade of his cavalry saber in a vicious sweep at the legs. The creature leaped like a ballet dancer, executing an impossibly high grand *jeté*, grinned, and came down ever so lightly. Then it charged like a Brahma bull, roaring, swinging its scimitar-shaped sword over its head like a helicopter blade.

"Die, mortal!" it bellowed.

Tom backstepped and stumbled over loose rocks. He snatched one up and hurled it at the demon. It hit the creature squarely in the nose. The demon stopped, dropped its sword, and screamed in anguish.

"You filth!" it screeched. "That's not fair!"

"Sorry, a human trick," Tom said. With a quick slash, he cut off the creature's head.

And promptly got two creatures, for his trouble.

"Damn," Tom said, spinning and running.

Now he faced three adversaries. Taking cover behind a hedgerow, he scanned the clearing and did a head count. Chagrined, he saw not three, but at least five medium-sized demons running about, and two more pint-sized ones.

"Marianne?"

"Here! The little devils keep splitting!"

She sprinted to him and dived behind the hedge. Tom helped her up. Together, they ran toward the lights and the music.

If there was a path through the dense thicket, it was not visible. They ran into a blind alley. Forced to retreat along their tracks, they found themselves in another leafy cul-de-sac.

"*Merde!*"

"This is getting boring," Tom exclaimed.

"Do you see them?"

"Maybe they buggered off."

Tom nearly choked on his words, for the demons had merged into one monstrously huge creature, at least three meters tall, with a sword proportionately large.

It stood blocking the path ahead.

In a gravelly voice, the demon warned, "None shall pass." Rows of wicked teeth glowed in the dark.

"No argument here," Tom said.

The creature took three steps forward. "First the female, then you. I will cut her to pieces while you watch."

Brandishing her sword, Marianne shouted, "*Foutre le camp, bête de Hadès!*"

"Spirited little filly, is she not?" the creature said with an indecent grin.

"Marianne, run!" Tom yelled, sprinting toward the demon, saber's point leading. He meant to spear the critter square in the breast and see what effect that had.

The big creature was slow to react, and Tom thought he had a fighting chance. If, that is, he could duck out of the way of the immense blade that was swinging toward the top of his skull.

Tom leaped. His blade sank into the creature's curiously pulpy thorax . . . The demon exploded in a flash of green flame. A loud report echoed through the wood.

Tom found himself upended in the bushes. He thrashed about before getting free with Marianne's help.

"Where'd he go?"

"*Je ne sair pas*," Marianne said, shrugging. "Gone, *pouf!*"

"Must have hit his detonator button or something. Jeez."

Tom saw Marianne stare toward the right, and followed her gaze. "Lord Auberon!"

"Good evening."

Auberon, Lord of the Seelie Court, stepped from the shadows, his long cloak flowing behind him. He was a handsome creature, tall, fully human in appearance except for strangely pointed ears. In his eyes was something quaintly eldritch, at once unearthly and empathetic.

If human eyes are windows to the soul, then Faerie eyes are mirrors of eternity. They seem to glow with a light all their own. Yet it was not spooky, Tom thought. It was a good light, a benevolent light, benign in some mystical way.

"You had a spot of trouble, I see."

"Did you do the fireworks?" Tom asked.

"I did," Auberon said.

"Thanks. We needed help."

"It was nothing. The creature was preoccupied. I do not think it detected my presence, until it was too late."

"Nevertheless, that was a pretty neat trick," Tom said, sheathing his sword. "I didn't know you were at the ball."

"I arrived late," Auberon said. He tossed Marianne the remains of her gown. "I believe you'll be wanting this, Countess."

"Thank you, Auberon," she said, gathering it up. "I'll never get it back together tonight. I think I will retire early. I am a mess."

"You look divine," Auberon said, unabashedly looking her up and down. Marianne did not mind. He was not human, and somehow, paradoxically, that made his stare seem not at all improper.

"Again, you have our undying thanks, Auberon," Tom said.

"Glad to be of help. I sensed an intrusion as soon as I arrived at the castle, but it took some time to locate the source. I'm glad I was not too tardy. One word of caution."

"Sure."

"You embark tonight upon a path fraught with danger. Tread it carefully. That is all I can say at the moment."

"Thanks."

Auberon turned. "I believe the way out lies in that direction. I will see you both later, I hope. Meanwhile, I think I will stroll about and make sure there are no other interlopers."

"Take care," Tom said over his shoulder. "And thanks again."

"Farewell." Auberon raised a hand before disappearing into the darkness.

Tom found the path, such as it was, and led Marianne from the bushes. They emerged just as a dowager duchess, lorgnette in hand, strolled along the pathway, escorted by an elderly, epaulet-heavy lancer general, doubtless in late retirement.

Raising her handled eyeglasses, the dowager took one look at the half-naked Marianne and stifled a scandalized shriek.

Tom caught back a yelp of his own. Goethe's body was gone.

"How do you figure it, Marianne?" he asked.

"I don't know," she said. "I saw him fall. You were nearer. Did he die?"

"I didn't stick around to make sure. He looked dead. The dagger was up to the hilt in the middle of his chest. Do you think there were more of them to carry the body off? But why?"

"It makes no sense."

"Maybe he's okay. Maybe he got up and walked away. But that doesn't make sense, either."

Marianne winced. "I have cuts all over my legs. See me to my room?"

"Sure."

"Brazen hussy!" the duchess hissed at their backs.

"Ah, to be young again." The general beamed.

CHAPTER 7

CITY OF LIGHT

As he rode the train to Paris the next morning, Tom puzzled over his conversation with Goethe. Something in that conversation bothered him, but for the life of him, he couldn't decide what it was. He believed it was something the agent had implied rather than stated outright. There was a nagging sense that everything Goethe said hadn't jibed.

Frowning, Tom admitted to himself that all the events of the previous evening were muddled in his mind.

Even more vexing was a communication through secret channels received by the Secret Service that morning, shortly before Tom left for Paris. The message—from Goethe himself, miraculously resurrected—had been addressed to Tom.

He drew it out to read again.

i

My dear Captain Olam,

You will doubtless be mystified by this note, but be reassured, I am quite all right. The knife wounded me only superficially, expending most of its energy in piercing my cigar case and its contents. The point of the blade lodged a few centimeters in my flesh, but for some curious reason did no great damage, except to let a little blood ruin a perfectly good boiled shirt. I am especially peeved about the gold cigar case, a family heirloom.

I made off before your return because someone was approaching and I did not want to create a scene. Thinking it wise, I left the castle immediately. I am ashamed to say that my seeming death was due entirely to my fainting from utter terror. A delicate and hysterical sensibility is something of a liability in a spy, but I am afraid I am cursed with exactly that. I will communicate with you further anon, by the usual method. Until then, please be assured of my highest regard, during which time I remain

Your humble servant,
"Goethe"

Tom downed his apéritif and sat back, watching the suburbs of Paris roll past the windows of the lounge car.

He was not satisfied with Goethe's message. It didn't ring true.

Maybe, the spy had run off in a panic, as he alleged. Maybe he had heard the sword fighting, smelled Unseelie, and hightailed off. But, by God, he had a knife buried in his chest. The whole thing just didn't ring true.

"*Monsieur?*"

Startled from his reverie, Tom glanced up to see a waiter. "Eh?"

"*Un autre, Monsieur?*"

"Uh . . . *non, merci.*"

Tom paid for his drink, then gazed through the window until the train pulled into the station. No one else interrupted him.

Paris.

Tom knew that the Paris of 1872, back in the "normal" universe, was the age of Napoleon III and the Empress Eugenie. It was the Paris of Manet, of Proust, of Degas, Zola, Monet, and Victor Hugo. Manet was painting Nana, the showgirl, while Zola was immortalizing her in a novel that would win acclaim, but not as much as Victor Hugo had garnered with his sprawling novels of social unrest. It was said that in Hugo's time, a letter addressed simply, "Hugo, France," would have been readily delivered. While Hugo painted his large-canvas novels, the Impressionists were exploring the latest word in painting, and the word was "light." Paris became the City of Light. It was a time of great literature and of even greater art. The Paris of 1872 reigned as the cultural capital of Europe.

But what about the Paris of "New Europa"?

The short answer: New Europa was Europe with more, and Paris was there every bit as resplendent as the "original."

Renovated in the 1860s by the architect and city-planner, Baron Haussmann, the city enjoyed wide, tree-lined boulevards radiating from numerous plazas, such as the central

Place de l'Étoile, home of the Arc de Triomphe. Tom saw this timestream's Paris as one of the most beautiful cities on earth, complete with art salons, bistros, sidewalk cafes, theaters, fashionable shops, cathedrals, stately homes, and grand apartment buildings.

But in New Europa, fiction and fact merged into a single reality. Jules Verne was a resident journalist, for what was fiction in another universe here became reportage. Robur the Conqueror, in his *Albatross,* plied the skies of the world and Captain Nemo, in his *Nautilus*, claimed the seas. While walking the streets of Paris, one might glimpse Phileas Fogg hurrying to catch a train to Calais, to connect with a packet to Dover.

You could look up and see a dragon in flight.

You might take a seat in a sidewalk cafe and find a Faerie individual sitting nearby.

Everything familiar was here as well: the Place de la Concorde, the Île de la Cité, the Tuilleries, the Place de la Bastille, Notre-Dame, the Louvre, and of course, cutting through it all, the Seine. There was no Eiffel Tower, for that landmark was yet to be built.

Whatever the universe, whatever was in it, Tom loved Paris.

Giroud—Libraire et Bouquiniste shared a block of less fashionable shops and low-rent art galleries in Montparnasse. Tom found the store all but deserted. Crowded bookshelves lined the walls while standing bookshelves covered the floor. Geroud's resembled the archetypal bookstore found in the bohemian sections of most cities of the world: it was somewhat disorderly and featured a wide selection along with a relaxed atmosphere redolent with the smell of old books. The obligatory bookstore cat, an orange tabby, greeted Tom, rubbing against his leg as he stepped up to the sales counter. He stooped to stroke its fur. It burbled, sniffed him, then padded away.

Tom rang a touch bell on the counter, but no one appeared. The shop remained quiet.

Literature seemed to be the focus downstairs. He browsed, then mounted creaky stairs to a loft, where he found more books, including many art portfolios. He saw signs here and there—Poetry—Popular Fiction—History—but no clue to the whereabouts of a monograph on rocketry. He peered down the stairs and saw a man smiling up at him.

The man spoke as Tom descended the staircase. "May I help you, Monsieur?"

In spectacles and an artist's smock, but lacking a beret, the man looked every inch the amiable book store proprietor, surely, M. Giroud.

"Yes," Tom answered. " Do you have any technical literature?"

Giroud's brow furrowed. "Technical literature, Monsieur?? Ah, well, that depends on what exactly you mean."

"I was specifically looking for something on the science of rocketry."

The man's face went blank. "Rocketry."

"Yes. Rockets. Building them. Firing them off. That sort of thing. Uh, you do understand?"

"Certainly, Monsieur. Rockets." Giroud chewed his lip pensively. "I am not quite certain . . ."

"Have you ever heard of a book on rocketry by a German named von Bremen?"

"Von Bremen," Giroud said, as if trying to remember. "Ah, von Bremen."

"You've heard of him, then."

"Ah . . ." The amiable expression saddened. "I regret to say, no, Monsieur."

"I'm looking for a specific work," Tom persisted, "von Bremen's technical monograph. Published in three volumes, limited edition. They might be boxed. Ever run across such a set?"

"Ahhhh . . ." The man searched his memory with apparent care. "What was the author's name again?"

Tom sighed. "Von Bremen. Karl Friedrich von Bremen."

The little man shook his head. "Never heard of him. Do you have the book's title, Monsieur?"

"No, sorry, I don't know the exact title."

The man threw up his hands in a Gallic shrug. "Then it is hopeless, Monsieur."

"Maybe, not," Tom said, refusing to be turned away. "Is a section of the store devoted to technical subjects?"

"Ah, which technical subjects would you be interested in, Monsieur?"

"Rocketry," Tom said, becoming exasperated. "Remember?"

"Ah, yes. Quite. Rocketry. Ah-hah."

Tom waited. The man said nothing more. "Well?"

"Well, what, Monsieur?"

"Where is your technical section?" Tom drew a calming breath and tried again. "Listen . . . how about military science? Von Clauswitz. That sort of thing."

"Military science!" Giroud clapped his hands. "*Oui,* Monsieur. In the basement."

"The basement?"

"Yes. We have a basement."

"I see." Tom glanced around. "Uh, where . . . ?"

"The door is in the back, Monsieur." Giroud gestured between aisles of bookshelves to a narrow, paneled door set into a far wall. "You see?"

"Got it. Thank you."

"Happy to serve you, Monsieur."

"If you don't mind, I'll browse a little, then check downstairs."

"Not at all, Monsieur."

Tom scanned several shelves toward the back. There were lots of interesting volumes. If he had more time, he would love to browse through this old store. He loved books, old books especially, and there were antiques here, beautifully leather-bound. Most of the titles were French, of course, but foreign languages were represented, even English. Wonderful rare editions might be gathering dust here, Tom mused. A first Byron or Shelley, perhaps. Maybe something really rare, like . . .

Movement at the corner of his eye alerted him to danger. He threw himself backward just in the nick of time. A towering, overloaded bookshelf slammed noisily to the floor, sending books flying. It missed him by a hairbreadth.

"Monsieur!"

Tom picked himself up and slapped at sawdust, lint and paper bits clinging to his dark suit. Hopeless. He took off his jacket.

"Are you all right, Monsieur?" The agitated proprietor wrung his hands together.

"Quite," Tom said, continuing to swat at the jacket.

"Never, never has that happened before! Why, it nearly stopped my heart. I thought you would be killed! Oh, that such a thing should happen in my store—!"

"Think nothing of it, M. Giroud," Tom said coolly. "It was close, but no harm's done."

"I would never forgive myself if such a calamity befell a customer."

Tom inspected the fallen case. Rusted antique nails protruded through the back. They had once been driven through the wood into the wall and had apparently picked that moment to pull out.

"You should go around with some proper nails and reinforce these taller cases," Tom warned. "And clear some of the extra weight off the shelves."

"That I will do, Monsieur! Certainly, absolutely—are you *quite* sure you're unhurt?"

"Take it easy. I won't sue."

This seemed to reassure the little man.

Tom's gaze moved up the wall to its junction with the floor of the loft. Someone hiding there might have given the case a little assist with a crowbar. He hadn't seen anyone upstairs, but the loft was expansive. Someone could have been hiding behind one of the freestanding cases up there.

Had he been so absorbed in rare titles that he missed the rasp of a crowbar against the old wood? Tom decided to put it all out of his mind. He dusted off his pants and made for the basement door. It creaked open at his touch. Beyond, a stairwell lit by tiny gaslights twisted into the bowels of the building. Tom began to descend, but at the fourth landing, he paused to wonder at the number of stories. The gaslights barely staved off total darkness.

"Cheery place," Tom said. "It's a wonder Giroud doesn't get a lawsuit now and then."

These stairs were killers, to boot, steep, with narrow, warped treads. Coming up might be more hazardous than going down.

A basement odor permeated upward, a mixture of mildew and dust, along with the unmistakable musk of earth that has not seen the light of day in years. All cellars smell the same, Tom mused. It was cooler, too. He pulled his jacket on.

At last, the staircase debouched into a cavernous underground room crammed with books: books everywhere, on sagging ancient shelves, piled in corners and against stanchions, stacked to the joists above, thrown into heaps, and moldering away in boxes and crates. There were tens of thousands of them.

Tom wandered among them. Obviously, this wasn't part of the store. This was overstock or stock that hadn't moved in fifty years and had been thrown down here. Something was fishy. Tom doubted that customers ever came down here.

Still, he had to assure himself that the monograph wasn't here. Maybe he should go up and talk with Giroud again. The man must have an inventory he could check. Surely, he had some idea which books were in his store and which were not.

Looking at this mess, though, Tom began to doubt it. Giroud seemed to be something of a flake. Then again, maybe the man wasn't Giroud, himself. He had implied that it was his store, but he might have recently bought out Giroud and not yet taken inventory.

Tom turned a few corners. The chamber seemed endless: many side passages radiated from it, all stuffed with cartons of books.

"It's like a huge rummage sale," he muttered.

He ducked into one tunnel-like passage, but decided not to follow it. When he retraced his steps, he nearly ran into a tall, beefy man with a thick, flat nose and a sneer on his porcine face. The fellow wore coarse workman's clothing and a slouch hat.

"What the hell are you doing down here?" he demanded.

"Just browsing," Tom told him.

"No customers down here. Not allowed."

"I was told by the proprietor that something I want might be in this part of the store."

"Nothing down here but junk." The man's tone became surly. "You have to leave."

"I was under the impression this was part of the store. The basement part. Mr. Giroud told me—"

"Who? You're leaving, friend." The man grabbed Tom by the lapels.

Tom brought his hands up sharply between the fellow's meaty forearms, breaking his hold, then followed with a quick right to the snout. The man staggered back a few steps.

"You must remember to keep your hands off the customers," Tom reminded him.

The thug rubbed his nose, shook his head, then charged. Tom sidestepped and whipped out with a karate kick to the kidney. The man crashed into boxes, sending books tumbling. It took him a while to pick himself off the dirt floor, but he charged again. This time Tom whumped him in the face with an unabridged dictionary. He added a chop to the back of the neck, for good measure.

Even that didn't put the guy out of commission. Like a downed elephant, he began laborious process of elevating himself to his feet.

Tom considered getting out his pistol. He didn't like the idea of shooting an unarmed man in cold blood, unless absolutely necessary.

Backing into an aisle between two freestanding wooden shelves, he reached for his shoulder holster.

From behind, someone caught him into a choke hold. Tom drove his right elbow back, heard a gasp, and whirled, throwing his right fist. It connected with a face. The owner fell back into darkness. Tom backed out of the aisle and was immediately set upon by the big thug, who locked him in a shoulder-wrenching full nelson.

The other man, a skinny twist of a street punk with a face like a weasel, burst from the aisle, and began delivering blows to Tom's chest and diaphragm. Tom kicked out, connecting with the punk's groin. As the skinny one howled, Tom leaped, swinging his legs upward to lock the big one's head in a knee grip. Top heavy, the beefy man fell against a mountainous stack. A cascade of books, shelves, papers, boxes, boards, and the odd can of screws crashed around them.

It took little time for Tom to sort himself out of the wreckage. But he was not quick enough to ward off an attack by a third tough, who came out of the gloom like a moving shadow. Tom got in a few punches before getting all tied up again with one thug holding him, while another worked his midsection. This time, he broke the holder's grip more easily, freeing himself in time to fend off an attack with a crowbar. After deflecting a skull-crushing blow, he delivered an incapacitating hand chop to the throat of the beefy guy. The thug went down, making gurgling and choking sounds.

The third assailant, a squat stevedore type with ape-wide shoulders, began incongruously to box in classical fashion. Tom jabbed a few times, dancing around, doing the Marquis of Queensbury routine, then tossed a book for diversion, and sidekicked the man in the stomach. The thug did not drop. Tom snatched up a board and broke it over his head. The man slumped to the floor.

Tom looked about the cellar. "Anybody else want to dance?" he called, finally pulling out his Derringer.

No one moved. "No more Mr. Nice Guy, fellas. Next one shows a face gets it shot off."

Out of a tunnel, like a bat, came the weasel-faced punk. Tom down and sent the pistol skittering under a pallet. Tom rolled with the guy once, twice, coming up against something hard. As thumbs gouged at his eyeballs, Tom tried desperately to free his right arm. He made it and punched the wiry twerp in the side of the head, twice, three times before he fazed him. Tom rolled, sprang to his feet, and got his small opponent in a behind-the-back double arm lock.

"Where's Hauptmann?" he demanded.

"Who?"

"You heard me. Is he here, or are you his local field rep? Talk, creep."

The man yelped as Tom forced both of his forearms in a painfully wrong direction.

"Talk or your shoulders get dislocated," Tom said through clenched teeth.

"I do not know what you are talking about, Monsieur! M. Giroud—ahhhhhh, that hurts!—said that someone was in the cellar making trouble." The punk back-kicked Tom's shin, hard. It hurt, but Tom brassed it out.

"*Merde!* Talk. Where is Hauptmann?"

"There is no M. Hauptmann here! Ahhhhhhhh!"

"All right, once again, where is your boss?"

"M. Giroud is upstairs!"

"Again. Who are you working for?"

"Ahhhhh! You are going to break my arm—"

"It's Hauptmann, isn't it? Goethe knew I was on the *Wagner*. How did he know if Hauptmann didn't survive to tell?"

"To hell with your bloody Hauptmann! I don't know what you're raving about! You—"

"Talk," Tom commanded, ratcheting the forearms upward. Something popped.

The twerp howled.

"Ooops," Tom said. "Sorry. Here, let me help you."

He swung the punk into a side tunnel, sending the fellow crashing and banging into shelves and precipitating another major bookslide.

Tom's right eye smarted. "Little bastard tried to blind me," he muttered, hoping the cornea wasn't nicked. He yelled a taunt up the stairs. "You'd better have liability, Giroud!"

"Damn." He rubbed his eye tenderly. "Little creep."

When his eye stopped burning, he turned to scan the shadows. Something slammed into the back of head. That was the last thing he remembered.

CHAPTER 8

THE MIRROR

Marianne stifled a burp and looked down at the remains of her *stracotto alla Fiorentina*, roast beef Florentine style in a light tomato and wine sauce, with penne pasta. She couldn't finish it. She looked guiltily at signora Zambelli, who smiled indulgently and murmured, "Like a sparrow."

They were indulging in another lavish Zambelli meal, this one in the Zambelli's quarters in Falkenstein. Again, the cook was the inimitable Berenice, who made do with the small kitchen in the apartment. The Zambellis had insisted on bringing her, claiming they were constitutionally incapable of eating German cooking.

Berenice had yet to show her face to Marianne. Of course Marianne hardly expected her to, social proprieties being what they were (the well-to-do were not in the habit of introducing the help to their guests), but she wanted to see this remarkable woman. Berenice could cook like a dream.

"You like the beef, *Contessa?*" Zambelli asked. "Is good, eh? But you must leave some room for the *zuccotto*. Chocolate cake with almonds."

Marianne gave a little, silent, internal groan. She would look like an airship if she ate with the Zambellis regularly. She usually grabbed meals on the fly, raiding the castle cellars for wine and cheese. She didn't like to make a fuss about eating. But with her French heritage, she did have a palette, and she did appreciate culinary artistry.

"Have you talked with Rhyme about the rocket, *Signore* Zambelli?" Marianne asked.

Zambelli looked unhappy. "He's . . . he's . . . how you say? . . . he is not polite to me."

Marianne laughed. "Don't pay him any mind. He's that way to everybody. His bark is worse than his bite, believe me."

Zambelli snapped his teeth together. "I give him a bite, that little *finocchio*, right on his *culo*, eh?"

Marianne and the children laughed, but La Signora took umbrage.

"*Ruggi! Come si grossolano!*"

There ensued a heated exchange between the couple in Italian.

"I'm no say nothing bad," the Signore protested. "No *bestemmia*. Forgive me, *Contessa*."

"Oh, that's quite all right," Marianne said. "So, you're not getting along? He won't tell you what he thinks of your rocket engine?"

"Hah, what engine? It is in pieces, all over, down in that . . . how you say it? In the dungeon! I get the chills when I go down there. All he says is, she no work. That's all he has to say to me. 'The rocket, she no work.' You know what I say? Eh? I say *Vafungul!*"

"*Ruggi!*" La Signora admonished. "In front of the children!"

Zambelli's face pinked over. "Please pardon me, *Contessa*."

Marianne giggled. Zambelli made her laugh.

"Shameful!" Signora Zambelli was not amused.

At that moment, the castle shook. The walls rocked back and forth, the table rattled, and bottles of wine fell over. A vase on the sideboard fell and shattered. Signora Zambelli screamed. The younger boys ducked under the table.

The shaking stopped. Zambelli rose, fork in hand, napkin still tucked into his collar. "*Madonna!* What was that?"

Marianne jumped to her feet and pulled the ripcord on her dress. The long full skirt fell away, revealing riding breeches, boots, sword, and a holster with a pistol. The sight stunned *Signora* Zambelli more than the shaking.

"I'm going to find out." Marianne yelled as she dashed from the room.

"I'm going with you!" Zambelli yelled.

"*Ruggi, carissimo, non!*"

Ruggiero Zambelli rushed from the dining room.

Marianne burst from the Zambelli's quarters, turned left, and dashed down the corridor, heading for the South Tower. Zambelli followed, barely able to keep up.

"Where are we going?" Zambelli yelled.

"To the dwarf!"

"The dwarf?"

Marianne had a hunch.

An ensconced candle at every turn lit the tower stairs, but the light was dim. Marianne and Zambelli descended fourteen levels as quickly as they could, both aware that once they started tumbling on the spiraling stairs, they might not stop till they reached bottom.

Fifteen levels. The cellar, at last. Marianne ran across a vaulted crypt to another stairwell, this one going straight down through bedrock to the sub-basement. She reached a landing, and beyond, a wide-open door. She rushed through to yet another flight of steps, these twisting into Rhyme's workshop.

Marianne halted midway down the stairs. Zambelli almost ran her down.

"What happened here?" Marianne exclaimed.

The place had shrunk to half its former size. Or so it seemed.

"What is the matter?" Zambelli could not see that anything was amiss, save that the place was a jumble of junk.

"The walls . . . the room. It's gotten smaller."

"Eh? This I do not understand."

"Neither do I. Rhyme?" Marianne took a few more steps down. "Rhyme, can you hear me?"

A groan came from beneath a pile of debris.

"Rhyme!"

Marianne ran down the stairs and began digging through the refuse. Zambelli helped. By the time they had the dwarf engineer nearly unearthed, Tarlenheim and two castle Guardsmen had arrived to help complete the task.

Rhyme was conscious. Although groggy, he appeared essentially unhurt.

"Rhyme, what happened?" Marianne asked.

"A bloody explosion, wasn't it?" The dwarf looked up and saw Marianne. His expression softened a bit. "I don't know."

"Are you all right?"

"Yes, I think so."

Rhyme hauled himself to his feet and looked around. He glared defiantly up at Tarlenheim. "What do you want?"

Tarlenheim glared back. "What's all this ruckus?"

"Oh, just an experiment." Rhyme turned toward the larger end of the chamber. His jaw dropped. "Damn, that's what happened. My sorcerous engine shifted from burn-stabilizing to invisibility. No wonder there was a blow up."

He walked toward the far wall. What was going on over there was difficult to grasp. Some type of visual distortion was taking effect.

"Wasn't this place, bigger?" Tarlenheim asked.

"There was a long workbench over there," Marianne said. "It's gone."

"No, it's not," Rhyme said. He continued walking toward the wall. Suddenly, he disappeared.

"What in blazes?" Tarlenheim took a few steps, stopped. "Where the devil did he go?"

"I'm still here. Keep your britches on."

A few moments later, the long workbench suddenly materialized, piled high with rocket engine parts. The chamber now appeared twice its former size. It was disorienting to witness.

"La sorceria!" Zambelli hissed, crossing himself.

"Precisely," Marianne said.

"What is going on?"

"Magic." Tarlenheim smiled, elated. "Apparently Rhyme Enginemaster has devised a machine that makes itself invisible."

"I did that long ago," Rhyme said. "What I was doing was adapting it to stabilize Zambelli's rocket engine."

"Where?" Zambelli asked, walking to the bench.

"Here. Right here." Rhyme pointed to the curious planetarium-like mechanism on the bench. "You find the exact settings on the armature, and it becomes any number of engines, all with different functions."

"This invisibility interests me," Tarlenheim said. "If we put one on an aerowarship, we will have a ship that cannot be spotted by ground observers!"

"Don't be so damned eager!" Rhyme snapped. "Obviously, I haven't perfected it yet, or haven't you noticed that it blew out the other half of the room? When the screen went up, there was some kind of concussion. I had the last setting rigged to click in with a timing device. I took cover in the other part of the room, expecting some blow up. But the effect starts with the outer edge of the sphere of invisibility. That I didn't anticipate. Stupidly."

"Well, yes, I see, of course," Tarlenheim said. "But you're obviously on the right track. When . . . ah . . . when do you think—?"

"Blast it all," Rhyme said hotly, "when are you beanpoles going to understand that I don't deal in timetables?"

"Sorry, sorry," Tarlenheim said, executing a left face and walking away as if deflected. He shook his head. "I didn't mean to bully you . . ."

He stopped, then turned back. "But look here, don't you understand what a boon this can be for military intelligence? To be able to fly enemy skies sight unseen, to observe what needs to be observed."

Tarlenheim paused to ponder. "Intelligence? Why, in principle you could move whole units without being observed by the enemy. You could infiltrate behind enemy lines and be at their tail without their ever suspecting—"

"Oh, blow it out your own rear."

Tarlenheim frowned ominously. "Now, see here, dwarf."

"You see here. I wasn't going to tell you about this thing until it was utterly and completely perfected. You don't want to monkey around with the contraption until it is. The shock nearly killed me, and I was expecting it. This is dangerous business. I won't be responsible for any loss of life caused by your pig headed insistence on rushing this thing into production! I just won't do it!"

Tarlenheim took a few deep breaths. He grunted. Then he shrugged. "You know best. In any event, tomorrow you will begin working with *Signore* Zambelli on the rocket project."

Rhyme pointed to the debris on the bench. "Didn't I just say I've already begun? The thing needs lots of work."

"Be that as it may," Tarlenheim continued stiffly, "you won't have time to waste on research. Good night." He turned and marched up the steps. The guardsmen followed at his heels.

Zambelli looked around the workshop. "Very interesting. You have many very interesting things here, Herr Rhyme," he said in his best German, in an apparent effort to take an entirely new tack.

"Don't 'Herr' me. That's for human folks."

Zambelli bristled but suppressed a retort. "Forgive me. Uh, let me say, I am very pleased to be working with such . . . uh, with . . . *il maestro*—."

"Dwarf," Rhyme said, fiddling with an apparatus on the bench. "I'm a dwarf."

"Yes. I did not mean . . . what I'm saying is . . ."

"I think *Signore* Zambelli was trying to pay you a compliment," Marianne said.

"I know. Thank you."

"All the dwarfs in Italy know about him," Zambelli said, clearly determined to be civil. "He is a big hero."

"Really," Rhyme said casually.

Marianne walked over to Rhyme and laid a hand on his shoulder. "Are you sure you're not hurt?"

"Oh, don't worry about me, pretty lady." He glanced up at her "I have something for you."

"You do?"

"Unless it broke. No, here it is, on the bench." Rhyme blew dust from the mirror. "This. Want it?"

"A mirror." Marianne accepted with pleasure. "It looks old."

"Very old, I suspect."

"Oh, my, it is very nice." Marianne turned the mirror in her hands. "An antique. I wonder what medieval lady owned it. A queen, perhaps."

The mirror was a trifle dark, but it served its purpose well enough. Marianne looked at herself, passing a hand through her luxuriant hair.

"Well, do you want it? I have no use for it."

"Why, yes, Rhyme. Thank you. Where did you get it?"

"Cousin of mine sent it. Don't know why, but I suspect he wants something in return, the weasel."

"Are you sure you don't want to keep it?"

"No. It's for a lady, and a pretty one."

Marianne smiled. For all his churlishness, the little creature could be adorable. "What a nice thing to say. You can't
fool me, Rhyme. Underneath all that nasty stuff, I can see
you for what you are."

Rhyme's face turned a deep shade of pink. "Oh, get away
with you."

Marianne laughed, resisting an urge to press a kiss to his
cheek. "Good night, Rhyme. And thank you very much for
the mirror."

"It's magic, by the way."

"What? A magic mirror! Rhyme, how wonderful. What
does it do?"

"The incantation is burned into the back of the frame.
See? Anyone can do it, you don't need to be a magician. The
magic is in the mirror. You recite this and the person you
want to talk to appears in the mirror. If the person is near
another mirror, any mirror or reflective surface, then the
person can see you, and you can converse as well."

"Remarkable!" Marianne took note of the incantation.
"Just by reciting this verse?"

"Yes. It might take a few repetitions. Try it out and see. I
don't like to fool with magic, myself."

"I will." She stroked her fingertips across the burned in
letters. "I'll try to call Tom."

"Tell me if it works."

"I will. Good night, Rhyme."

"Good night, pretty lady."

Marianne gave in to impulse and touched his cheek,
lightly, with one finger. Rhyme's blush reblossomed.

Laughing, Marianne mounted the stairs. Zambelli followed.

CHAPTER 9

PARIS UNDERGROUND

Tom awoke in darkness. Rather, in semidarkness. A dim oblong of luminescence defined an ill-hung door. By the light leaking through, he could make out that he was in a small room. A storeroom, probably. He turned his head to see yet more cartons of books. He was lying on sacks of something fairly soft. The musty, deep cellar smell made breathing unpleasant.

He hurt. First and foremost, his head hurt, but pain flared everywhere. The thugs had worked him over good. His face hurt like hell and his ribs ached. He tried to move and convinced himself that nothing was broken or dislocated; but he was trussed up like a roast, his legs bent at the knees, his hands tied to his ankles. He could barely wriggle.

As his eyes adjusted to the light, he saw that this was indeed a storeroom, one filled mostly with crates of books and piles of heterogeneous junk.

Something else was in the room.

A pair of eyes.

They didn't look ghostly. They were human eyes, Tom decided. They floated in the shadows near the door, looking at him dispassionately but without malevolence.

"Hello," Tom said.

"Hello," a male voice replied.

"Uh . . . looks like we're prisoners together." Pain flared in Tom's jaw when he spoke. He wished he could rub it.

"Yes. Were you a customer?" the other man asked. His accent was not German, although it was close.

"Yes. And you?

"I came in to browse. This is my favorite bookstore. A strange man was at the counter, and I asked about M. Giroud, the proprietor."

"You know M. Giroud?"

"Oh, yes, for three years; for as long as I have been going to the Sorbonne. I asked the strange man what had become of M. Giroud, but wasn't satisfied with the answer. When I expressed concern, I was set upon by three hoodlums, who spirited me down to this hellish place. They bound me and locked me in this room. I've been here for hours."

"Maybe they did the same with M. Giroud."

"Do you know him, too?"

"Never met him. I just got to Paris this morning."

"You have an accent, if you'll pardon my saying so. Are you English?"

"Close."

"Do you speak Dutch, by any chance?"

"No. My German is pretty good, but not great."

"Then may we speak English? It is not my best tongue, but the roughs who attacked me were French, and they could be listening. I doubt they know English."

Tom was always glad to speak his native tongue. "Good idea."

"Fine. Allow me to introduce myself. I am Abraham van Helsing, a post doctoral student at the Sorbonne." Van Helsing spoke English with a pronounced British accent.

Now more accustomed to the gloom, Tom managed to pick out features besides eyes. He saw a young man with a pleasant face and an enormous head of hair that would be red in full light. So this was van Helsing, Bram Stoker's Dr. van Helsing of *Dracula* fame, come to life out of fiction.

Tom was surprised, but not inordinately so. In New Europa, fictional characters had a way of popping up. He suppressed an urge to let on that he had heard of the world's most famous vampire hunter, as that would be hard to explain. This was a young van Helsing, years before he achieved his notoriety at that dangerous sport.

"Pleased to meet you," Tom said. "Did you happen to learn who's in charge of this charade?"

"I heard the name Moriarty mentioned."

"Moriarty!"

"I see you know something of the underworld," van Helsing said. "A very dangerous man, Moriarty."

"One of the most dangerous," Tom agreed. "But it figures. His World Crime League freelances for foreign governments. This is just the kind of operation he would run."

"What exactly is his present operation, as you call it?"

"I can't really go into it just now." Tom tugged against his ropes, wishing he could rub his multiple bruises. "I'll only say there is something here that certain foreign governments want."

"I presume you are an agent of one of those governments."

"No use my denying it, Dr. van Helsing."

"I appreciate having a doctorate conferred on me, but it is premature," van Helsing corrected. "I hope to have my degree in another year or two. I do have a degree in medicine, but that is not quite the same as being a *philosophe*, a true scholar. I did not catch your name, Mister . . . ?"

"Sorry. Olam, Tom Olam. And since you are an M.D., may I call you Doctor?"

"If you wish. Olam! Of course. The Man out of Time. I am happy to meet you, Mr. Olam. You are allied with the Bavarian throne, are you not?"

"That's right." Tom shifted, and despite his aching ribs, managed to maneuver one hand along his boot. "Call me Tom. Are you tied up?"

"Quite securely, hands and feet, though I have been scraping the rope against a rusty nail point protruding behind my back."

"Any results?"

"Not a great deal, I am afraid."

"Well, let's apply a little scientific rigor to the experiment. And a sharper edge."

A curious *click* sounded in the darkness.

"What was that?" van Helsing asked.

"I have a switchblade built into the toe of my right boot. Can you turn around?"

"I think so." Tom heard the scrape of movement against stone. "There."

"Carefully, find the blade, then cut your ropes," Tom instructed, bending his wrist to hold out the blade. "Mind you, don't slice a wrist. It's as sharp as a razor."

"Than is an interesting device?"

"Comes in handy. Can you locate it?" Tom tried to inch forward. "I can't move very well."

Van Helsing shifted position, then grunted. "Ah, here it is."

"Careful."

"Rest assured. It cuts like a Saracen sword . . . just a moment . . . there!"

Van Helsing's ropes dropped. After a moment of sorting things out, he made short work of freeing Tom. "What now?" he asked.

Tom stood, grunting as his bruised ribs complained. Crossing the storeroom, he checked out the lock on the door. "Now, with the aid of a little chemistry, we get out of here."

He sat down and again reached for his boot.

"Most interesting." Admiration filled van Helsing's voice. "Those boots of yours are a veritable storehouse of resources."

"This lump of stuff," Tom said, removing a puttylike substance, "is an exotic explosive."

"Stored in the heel of your boot? Is that not dangerous?"

"Percussion won't detonate this stuff. In fact, it won't explode so much as go up in a very hot flame, very quickly. It's a magnesium compound with a fast oxidizer. It should make short work of this lock and without much of a sound."

Tom worked the substance with his fingers, then stuffed it into the keyhole. Next, he detached a length of cord from behind his jacket lapel and affixed that to the putty. From behind the other lapel, he took a match, or a "lucifer," as it was called these days.

"Get back, and cover your eyes. This will be bright enough to sear the retina."

"As you say."

Tom first put his ear to the door. Satisfied there was no one in the immediate area, he stepped back, struck the match, and lit the fuse. Retreating to the other corner, he hid his face.

After a sputtering hiss, the room lit up, the incandescence so brilliant that even the reflection from the dank walls dazzled the eyes.

The light faded. Darkness returned, though now it was mitigated by light leaking through a door thrown ajar. A neat hole, smoking and dripping with molten metal, let in more light where the lock had been.

Tom eased the door open and poked his nose out. The storeroom was apparently located in one of the side passages off the main basement. Edging out a little and looking to the right, he decided the main room lay in that direction. He decided to head left and ty to find a back way out. There must be a loading dock or freight entrance, or at least stairs to the back alley.

"Let's go," he told van Helsing.

They made their way down the dark passage, skirting the inevitable piles of book-filled crates. The floor of the tunnel slanted down gradually. Tom wondered how far below street level it ran before it reached an exit.

Faint light seeped through an opening in the wall ahead, a recent excavation, from the look of it. The tunnel went only about two yards before breaking through into an immense chamber with an underground river gurgling through it. An unmistakable smell gave it away.

"The sewers!" van Helsing said.

"Amazing. So that's how Moriarty's gang gets around Paris."

Van Helsing approached two vessels moored at the river's edge. "What are these strange conveyances, do you suppose?"

Tom joined him and inspected the two curious boats, flat-bottomed and compact. They sported two sets of wheels, front and back, canted at an outward angle. Blades formed the spokes, creating paddlewheels. The components of a miniature steam engine crammed the stern of each vessel. Wisps of steam trailed from safety valves on the boilers.

Tom grasped the principle almost immediately. "Sewer buggies," he said. "Amphibious automotives. These propellers serve as wheels when the water is too low. See how they're slanted? Fits nicely against the curving walls."

"Ingenious," van Helsing said. "Who do you suppose constructed them?"

"Moriarty had them built, I'd be willing to bet. Let's see if we can't hot-wire one."

"Eh?"

"Steal one. Get in, *Herr Doktor*."

"Again, you seem to know what you're doing. Very well, *mein Herr*."

Of course there was no hot-wiring to be done, as the controls were all mechanical. The boiler had almost a full head of steam. Tom had scarcely turned up the coal-oil flame when a needle on the pressure gauge climbed into the "Operational" range. All that remained was to screw up the wicks on small lanterns mounted to brackets on the gunwales. The lanterns threw light forward and to the sides.

A handle engaged the clutch, while a wheel controlled the rudder. Tom pulled out the clutch. The propeller-wheels began to turn. Tom eased the boat toward the middle of the channel, and they were on their way.

He had no idea of where they were headed. Anywhere out in the wider sewer system, away from the port of Giroud, was okay with Tom.

"Look for a ladder to a manhole," he advised van Helsing.

"I shall." Van Helsing looked over the side. "This channel appears deep. I had no idea there were veritable rivers of sewage underground. But I should have known that the sewers of Paris would surpass anything ever built by the Romans, even the great Cloaca of Rome, itself."

"I wouldn't count on the water staying this deep. We may have to test this buggy's overland capability before long."

"A truly ingenious device. I would pay my compliments to the inventor if I did not know what a villain he is. This device could not have been magicked together for anything but an ignoble purpose."

"I fear you're right, Dr. van Helsing." Tom considered. "Tell me, what's the weather been like the past few days?"

Van Helsing surveyed the shadows and shivered. "A most disquieting place. I beg your pardon? The weather. Forgive me, but I'm not up to making small talk at the moment."

"I had a reason to ask. Has it rained in the last week? That could affect the water level."

"What a dunce I am. Of course, I'm truly sorry. Let me see. I do believe it did rain last week. This week, no. Not much, in any case."

"The Seine appeared to be about normal height. That means the water level here should be the same. But we need to get out as soon as possible. A sudden cloudburst could be trouble down here."

"A worrying thought." Van Helsing scanned the walls. "Yet I see no way out at the moment."

"Let's put on some speed. I assume this is the throttle."

Tom pulled another handle. The miniature steam engine began chugging. The boat picked up speed, its paddle-wheels churning the odoriferous water.

"Remarkable, this contraption," van Helsing said. "I realize I said I was not disposed toward chatting, but I can't help wondering what this hugger-mugger is all about. My guess . . . and it's only a guess, is that the object of the chase is a book. Pardon my idle curiosity, but this I find intriguing. Am I at all close to the truth?"

There was little use in denying it. "It must be fairly obvious it has something to do with a book."

"Or books. I won't ask you which one, but it so happens I am the greatest of bibliophiles myself, the rarer and more arcane the tome, the better. I have a penchant for obscure works on the occult, in particular. I have been know to traverse the length and breadth of New Europa on a quest for a *grimoire* or treatise on necromancy."

"This isn't about magic, not in the ordinary sense, at least."

"Ah. If it were, I might offer to lend a hand."

"Perhaps you could help, Dr. van Helsing," Tom said. "If you were after a surpassingly rare volume, where would you look?"

"Well, there are any number of old libraries I'd search first. To mention one, the library of the Benedictine monastery of Corleto. A remote and godforsaken place. Many a volume thought lost to the ages has turned up in Corleto."

"How about something more recent? Of a technical nature."

"A technical nature? There are about a dozen book collectors whom I'd try first."

"No stores?"

"Ah, I'm afraid stores are of no use. Anything truly rare is bought up almost the instant it goes on sale. I'm talking about private collections in and about the continent. And in the British Isles."

"Names?"

"Well . . . there is a certain British lord . . . Ashton Montague, I believe is his name."

"One of the Steam Lords. No help there."

"Ah, I see, too political a choice. Well, now. There is the private library of the Elector of Saxony. And that of a baron in Saxe-Coburg. Hmmm. Let me think. There is an Austrian fellow. I seem to have forgotten . . . let me think."

"Take your time." Tom raised his head. "Do you hear something?"

An indeterminate echoing seemed to follow them.

"Why . . . I believe so."

"Someone's after us. In the other amphibian. I'll turn here."

The channel branched into a Y ahead, and Tom steered right.

The new channel was slightly narrower. Tom pushed the throttle forward another notch. The steam engine's chug-chug turned into a steady thrum. The engine's operation was extremely smooth. Tom could hardly believe that a steam engine could approach such sophistication.

The pursuing echo grew louder. Something was definitely following. Tom looked back and saw the other sewer buggy in hot pursuit, several men manning it, perhaps four crowded together. That second boat may have more seating capacity. It appeared to be faster.

We may have heisted the wrong buggy, Tom thought glumly.

Too late to stop and get out. It was going to be tricky to get away with four men chasing them.

Tom pushed the throttle to its extreme forward position.

"They seem to have a faster boat," van Helsing said.

Tom scanned the small control panel and saw another control rod. "Here goes nothing." He pulled it out. The boat suddenly slowed.

"Whoops."

A loud report sounded behind. A shot whizzed by their ears.

"Have they no sense of fair play?" van Helsing said indignantly. "We are unarmed!"

"That's the way they like it," Tom said.

He pushed the rod back in, guessing that it changed the pitch of the blades on the propellers.

"No way we can outrun 'em," he conceded.

"I think they will overtake us soon," van Helsing shouted.

"Do you have more miraculous devices in that wonderful boot of yours?"

"Nope, in my coat." Tom withdrew a small black sphere with a length of string dangling from it. "Pull that string."

Van Helsing pulled, and the string came away. Smoke rose through a tiny hole. Tom threw the thing into the air. It fell into the water behind the boat. They heard a popping sound, then a column of smoke billowed from the water. Tom and van Helsing threw three more smoke devices. The channel grew thick with a choking, greenish fog.

"That'll slow 'em awhile," Tom yelled.

He pulled back the throttle and swerved into a side channel. They made their way up this for about fifty yards. The water level began to get shallow.

"Heading away from the river," Tom explained.

"I think we've lost them."

"We'd better find a hatchway up and out of here, and soon."

The glimmer of lantern light from the boat showed only bare walls and little of that. "What positively Stygian darkness," van Helsing said.

They both clutched their seats as the boat bumped aground. It did not stop. The paddlewheels became tires that bore the strange hybrid craft along the circular sewer channel, rolling over concrete and stone, making quite a din. For all that, the ride was smooth.

Somebody needs to invent rubber tires, Tom thought, wincing at the noise.

They came to another fork, and this time Tom decided to take the left, as the right looked a little claustrophobic. He wanted maneuvering room.

Without warning, the other sewer buggy came out of a side channel, guns blazing.

Tom swerved, went up on the curving bank, and came back down again. Another side tunnel lay ahead. He raced for it as bullets whistled past.

"Get down, *Herr Doktor!*" Tom yelled.

Van Helsing needed no prompting, already having flattened himself against the bottom of the boat.

"How did they find us?"

"Moriarty knows his Paris sewers," Tom said.

In the next hectic minutes, Tom made turn after turn, becoming completely lost. An idea came to him. He turned down the lantern wicks. Light filtered from somewhere, possibly daylight leaking through vents. But where the hell were the manholes? Didn't all sewers have access points for sewer maintenance workers?

Certainly, but try to find one when you need one. Incongruously, flashes of an old movie ran through Tom's mind. Neither could Harry Lime couldn't find a manhole as he fled from the British through the sewers of post–Second World War Vienna. Was he in this universe, too, with all the other fictions?—rather, would he be here, when it got to be the twentieth century?

Maybe not. If Tom had anything to do with it, there would never be a World War Two. Nor a Holocaust, nor the atomic bombing of Hiroshima, nor the millions of deaths and the ensuing tension of the Cold War. He was here to prevent those tragedies.

Wonder if Harry Lime looks anything like Orson Welles, Tom mused, before his attention was caught by the sound of rushing water. He sensed approaching doom.

He didn't know what form the doom would take, but something was ahead. Now he heard an echoing, gurgling, and splashing, along with a steady babble of . . . what, rapids? No.

A spillway.

"Interesting," Tom said with numb detachment, as the boat nosed toward an incredibly steep incline, sluiced by sheets of water.

Van Helsing yelled, "*Herrgott!*" and continued yelling all the way down. When the boat/buggy hit a small lake below, sending up high plumes of smelly water, he sprawled across the bottom of the boat, still swearing oaths and promising to reform if permitted to live.

"Better than Pirates of the Caribbean," Tom said.

"I beg your pardon?"

"Looks like we lost them temporarily."

As if on cue, the pursuing boat/buggy came sliding down another concrete chute, hitting the lake with a towering splash. In a moment, bullets erupted from it, spatting into the water inches from Tom's side.

"Hell," Tom said.

The boat/buggy's centrifugal clutch abruptly disengaged.

"Damn!" Tom leaped from his seat, brushing by the Dutch physician and nearly pushing him overboard. He set upon the engine, frantically prodding, thumping, and jiggling the clutch linkage that connected the cam shaft with the belt drives that turned the propellers.

"Van Helsing, throttle her up!"

"Pardon?"

"Push the throttle all the way up!"

"Oh . . . this?"

"*Défense de tirer!*" a deep, raspy baritone called from the approaching boat "Well, well, Mr. Olam, I was wondering when our paths would cross again."

"I've been counting the hours, Moriarty," Tom said, continuing to fiddle with the linkages.

"I've been hearing rather a lot about you and your exploits. Some of them are quite extraordinary."

"Nothing extraordinary about me, Moriarty."

"On the contrary. I'm thinking you've a bit of the Faerie in you, what with all this blather about coming from another world and another time. From the future, no less, or so they say. Are you having a spot of mechanical trouble?"

"A bit," Tom said. "Nothing much. I've almost got it fixed."

Moriarty looked about his watery domain. "A fine thing, isn't it, to be mucking about in this filth? French filth, at that. But this is my empire, down here. My world."

Moriarty and his crew came abreast of the stalled boat. Moriarty, stern-faced and dark-eyed, looked pretty much as Tom had imagined him in fiction, though this was a much younger Moriarty than the one who would wrestle Sherlock Holmes over the Reichenbach Falls in the 1890s. Despite his young face, something anciently feral, almost reptilian, glinted in those dark eyes—even at a distance and even in this gloom.

"Well, never you mind about that engine, Mr. Olam. One of my men will take your boat back. Why don't you and your physician friend climb aboard Charon's ferry, here? Take care you don't fall into the Styx. Now, just come out from behind that engine—watch it! Get your hand out of that jacket! What's that you have there?"

"As the French say, *un petard*," Tom said, grinning. "Grenade."

From within his jacket, he drew a lighted black sphere, its fuse hissing and sparking. He tossed it into the middle of Moriarty's boat, where it rattled around, sputtering ominously.

"*Putain!*"

"*Zut!*"

All three henchmen dove into the gamy water. Moriarty sat alone, abandoned and scowling, as if oblivious to the danger at his feet.

In that moment, the clutch kicked in. The stalled boat lurched forward. Van Helsing reeled backward against the boiler, striking his head. Tom just stopped himself from being thrown off the stern. He scrambled forward.

A confluence of channels led into the lake, but only one led out. At the far end of the cavernous chamber, a huge pipe drained the lake of sewage. Tom headed for it at top speed. The boat was about to enter the pipe when the grenade exploded. Tom turned his head at the last second to see a ball of flame. It was impossible to judge Moriarty's fate.

The drain pipe tended down, gradually at first, then sharply, becoming another long, amusement-park slide. At the bottom, the pipe leveled off, but the water rose higher. The boat floated toward the top of the conduit. Tom ducked his head. Then he dived for the gunwales as boat and engine scraped the overhead, throwing sparks. The water boiled and bubbled. This is it, Tom thought, we'll be drowned

Churning, rushing water overwhelmed them. The boat began tumbling. Then like a clap of thunder, daylight exploded.

Tom felt himself free-falling through space, separated from the boat. He struck water with a hard smack and plunged into the depths of the river Seine.

Partially stunned, he kicked and thrashed toward the surface. Everything seemed to be moving in slow motion. Something blocked his way. A body—*van Helsing!*

Grabbing the sinking man, Tom strained toward the rippling surface just above; the blurry images of trees and quiet riverbank wavered over him.

Gasping, he broached the surface. He slapped van Helsing's face. The Dutchman's eyelids fluttered.

"Can you swim?"

"Eh? What? . . . Yes, I think."

It was not far to shore. They swam to a stone quay, and rested a spell, treading water. Presently, Tom found the strength to climb out of the river; he then helped van Helsing. Exhausted, they sprawled on warm stone in the sunlight.

Tom raised his head and looked out over the river. Nope, no pursuit, not that he expected any after the *pétard* had done its hoisting, so to speak.

There was no trace of the boat/buggy. It must have sunk.

"How's your head, van Helsing?"

"It hurts like the bloody devil. What in heaven's name happened?"

"I'll tell you all about it over a stiff drink."

"That sounds capital. Tell me, how did you do that lighted bomb trick?"

"Does an illusionist reveal his secrets?"

"Ah. Of course not."

"*Messieurs?*"

Tom tilted his head back to see a helmeted gendarme standing over him, twirling a nightstick. The face was vaguely, strangely familiar.

"I am sorree, bot zere eez naw swammeeng een ze reevaire. Eet eez agay-nest zee leuw."

Tom said, "I beg your pardon?"

"Eet eez agay-nest ze leuw."

"Against the what?"

"Ze leuw. *Ze leuw!* Do you not unnerstand-eh your own language?"

"Oh, the *law*. Yes, of course, sorry, constable. Er, we were just leaving."

"Silly English fools, to swim in zat durr-tee wahtaire. You should be asham-ed."

Tom got up, a little abashed. "Pardon me, constable. Uh, your name wouldn't happen to be . . . um . . ."

The gendarme turned. "*Oui*, Monsieur?"

"Uhhhh . . . nothing. Nothing. Sorry."

"Ver-ah well, *Monsieur*. Good day to yeu, then."

A soggy Van Helsing hauled himself unsteadily to his feet.

"You say you do this for a living?" he asked dubiously.

Tom said, "Yes. Why?"

"Some lofty, unseen Power must be absolutely enchanted with you."

CHAPTER 10

WE MUST TO ENGLAND

After spending an hour in the hotel's Turkish bath, Tom risked a two-hour nap, and woke unmolested, though tired and cranky. The stink of the sewer and river was still about him. It could have been his imagination, but he wanted another bath. He settled for a wash-up and a shave.

He was rummaging in his travel satchel when he heard Marianne's voice, as clear as day. "Tom, are you there?"

He straightened up. Maybe he'd gotten conked on the head, and was having audial hallucinations?

"Tom, can you answer?"

"Marianne?" Tom said, baffled.

"Here, in the mirror."

"What?"

He looked into the mirror over the washbasin, and there she was, smiling at him.

"What gives?"

She laughed. "Rhyme gave me a magic mirror."

"Are you kidding?"

"No. It works."

"Where are you?"

"At the castle. In my room. I have the mirror standing on my dressing table."

"Absolutely amazing. I had no idea you could do magic."

"I can't. All I have to do is recite this cryptic incantation. It's in Latin. Then I concentrate on the person I want to speak with, and . . . well, it took two or three tries."

"Pretty damn good," Tom said, marveling. "That thing is going to come in mighty handy for field communication. Where'd Rhyme get it?"

"From a cousin, he said."

"Cousin? Which cousin, did he say?"

"No. Does it matter?"

"I dunno. Dwarfs don't usually give things away. You might look into it. Meanwhile, I guess there's no harm in using it."

"Why would there be? I can keep track of you this way, make sure you don't get into any trouble." Her smile tilted. "I rather like you au naturel, *mon cher*. Where are you?"

Face heating, Tom moved closer to the sink. "In my hotel. Ran into some trouble at Giroud's. Something's brewing. I thought it might be the dead hand of Hauptmann, but it was Moriarty behind it all. At least in Paris."

"Moriarty?" Marianne repeated, sobering. "What does he have to do with the Prussian government?"

"I think he's freelancing. The Giroud bookstore was a

trap, and I walked right in. I think the Prussians hired Moriarty to do the job. I did find out that Moriarty runs his Paris operations from the sewers. Has a nifty little transportation system down there."

"Sounds dangerous," Marianne said. "And smelly. Are you hurt?"

"Not a bit. A little tired, though."

"Take care of yourself. By the way, I have to give you a communication from Goethe."

"Him again. What's he want this time?"

"He says he can arrange for you to visit a certain Viennese official who has a library—"

"No way! No more used book hunts for this kid. I think we can assume that the Prussians will be waiting for me when I get to Vienna."

"Goethe must have turned double agent?"

"I think he just might have been one all along," Tom said. "Anyway, I'm not taking any more chances. I'm fairly certain that the only way Goethe could have found out that I was aboard the *Wagner* that day was through Hauptmann. Can you think of another way?"

"You mean Hauptmann is alive?"

"Maybe—damn—you know, we can't be sure. We can't be sure that Goethe is a double, and we can't be sure that Hauptmann isn't dead. But I'm going to assume that Goethe is, and Hauptmann isn't. In any event, no Vienna for me. Like the cakes, *j'aime la valse*, but not this weekend."

Tom swung around at a knock on the door.

"Hold the phone . . . I mean . . . Jeez, this is kinda spooky, isn't it?"

"Spooky? You keep using those words I don't know."

"*Outré.* Hold on."

Tom whipped a towel around his middle, then cautiously opened the door. A bellhop stood outside. He offered a sealed envelope. "For you, Monsieur."

Tom tipped him from coins he'd dropped on the dresser, closed the door, and broke the seal.

"Just got a note from Dr. Abraham van Helsing," he explained to Marianne.

"Van Helsing? Should I know him?"

"No, not yet."

"Not yet? Tom, sometimes you . . . I don't know the word, either . . . you give me a headache. What do you mean, not yet? Tom, *mon cher?*"

Tom looked up from the note. "Huh? Sorry. He's a guy I met down in the sewers. Says he has an invitation to a weekend do at the estate of Lord Ashton Montague. Wants me to come along. This could be a break, Marianne. It just may be possible that Montague's steam engine factories are turning out rocket engines for the Prussians. Or at least fabricating them from Prussian plans."

He looked back at the note. "Van Helsing says Lord Montague might have the von Bremen books we want. As long as I'm there, if there are any plans, I can either steal them or find out where he keeps them."

"But you'll be recognized."

"Maybe. I'll have to come up with a disguise. I'm not all that well known in Britain yet."

"Still, it's a very big risk," Marianne said.

"We're in the risk business, *ma chérie.*"

"You're right, but be careful. Don't fall into any more traps."

"I trust van Helsing. I don't think he was planted in that storeroom to lead me to England. Anyway, I'd rather go to England than to Vienna."

Marianne chewed her lower lip. "Even so, I will use the mirror to check on you."

"How will you know where I am?"

"I don't have to know. The mirror will find you. Just make sure your room at the lord's manor has a mirror."

"Is that all? What a really neat device. Okay. See you later, dollface."

"I wonder how I am supposed to break the spell." Marianne peered around the frame. "It does not say. Maybe I should repeat the incantation? But I don't see how—"

Marianne's image suddenly vanished from the mirror. Tom was left staring into his own face.

"That's how," he said, laughing. "It's like a pay phone, *cherie*. You ran out of quarters."

The chalk cliffs of England, glimmering and vast, hove to in the distance. Tom had met van Helsing on the train to Calais, where both boarded an early evening packet bound for Dover.

The English Channel was calm tonight, the tide full, the moon lying close to the water—on the French coast, far away, daylight gleamed, and was gone.

Van Helsing and Tom stood at the rail of the main deck, looking out to sea.

"How comes it you know Lord Montague?" Tom asked.

"He is an amateur antiquarian. He wrote me a letter concerning a paper on Egyptian magic which I had published in a scholarly journal. I have corresponded with him over the last two years. A few months ago, he expressed an interest in an artifact I brought back from my last trip to the Near East. His invitation was in my post box when I got home. I thought you might be interested."

"Indeed I am. But I'll need a cover story."

"A which?"

"Something to explain my presence."

"I can say you are a colleague."

"Might work," Tom agreed. "But it would still be crashing the party."

"The invitation said I might bring one guest."

"Then it should be okay."

"As for posing as my colleague; do you know anything of antiquities, Egyptian or otherwise?"

"Pyramids and stuff? Not a whole lot. Except, you know, the usual. Tutankhamen, that sort of thing."

Van Helsing's brows elevated. "You know about such obscure matters?"

"Well, I thought everybody—"

Ooops. Anachronism, again. Tom silently berated himself for talking about something—the discovery of the boy pharaoh's tomb—that would not happen for fifty years. He did not know offhand if there was a Lord Carnarvon in this universe to discover it.

Van Helsing went on, "Antiquarians have for years debated the question of the location of the tomb of King Tutankhamen, who, as you must know, was surely one of the most inconsequential of the kings of Egypt. Nevertheless, his tomb has never been found, and it might be the only one that has escaped the depredations of tomb robbers. Alas, the site has been lost for millennia."

"I could pose as an expert on it. Believe me, I know more about it that anyone in this . . . well, anyone."

"Interesting. I would be fascinated to have any new light shed on the subject."

"So, you know about Egyptian magic," Tom said, shifting the subject from himself.

"The occult is a matter in which I am most interested, particularly the myths and legends of the dead. And the undead."

"Undead. Right, vampires."

Van Helsing's brow furrowed. "You are a strange man, if you don't mind my saying so. I would venture that few people know about the matters we have been discussing. Yet, to you, they seem to be familiar concepts."

"My knowledge of vampires is limited," Tom said. "I have met my share of spooks, though. Who hasn't, in this world of Faerie, dragon, and unicorn?"

"True, but the vampire is rare. And it is not the only species of the undead."

"Okay," Tom said, getting back to the matter at hand. "The upshot is that I pose as a fellow grad student at the Sorbonne. That's our story?"

"That is our story. I think we will be believed."

Tom watched the approaching shoreline as the packet headed into Dover Bay. "Let's hope so."

CHAPTER 11

RHYME AND ROCKETS

Rhyme ate everything the Zambellis had put in front of him. He especially liked the sage sausage, consuming link after link, washing it down with an excellent Italian beer.

When he pushed his plate aside, at last, his host invited him into the study. Zambelli spread out rolls and rolls of engineering schematics for the *Bomba Grossa Numero Due*, his idea of an advanced, improved rocket ship. While similar to the prototype in shape, it was about four times bigger.

Rhyme studied *Numero Due* with great interest and care, poring over huge sheets that crawled with drawings, charts, graphs, figures, and diagrams.

"So this whole rear assembly drops off at a certain altitude?" he asked, pointing.

"That's right," Zambelli said. "She drops off, falls to the ground."

"What if it hits something?"

Zambelli shrugged. "It fall in the mountains."

"Not the way I see it." The dwarf traced a stubby fingertip over a graph. "From the trajectory you have here in the flight plan, the rocket will crash somewhere in Bulgaria."

Zambelli looked over Rhyme's shoulder and clucked. "Not so good."

"Not so good," Rhyme repeated, his voice rising. "You can't go dropping rocket casings on people's heads."

"*Ma, si*, it can't be avoided," Zambelli insisted.

"The hell, it can't." The dwarf scowled at the schematics. "If you didn't drop anything off your rocket, you wouldn't have the problem."

"But *Signore* Rhyme . . . the mathematics of the rocket, she is . . . how you say, not forgiving! She says that you can't do it in one step. You need at least three steps in your rocket, or the rocket, she no go nowhere."

"I understand, but wouldn't it be better to build a one-step rocket?"

"*Ma*, sure! Sure, one step, she's better than three, or four, but *la matematica* . . ."

"To hell with mathematics. "What you need is a more efficient rocket engine. You gotta use magic."

"No magic! No work of the devil!"

"Oh, for pity's sake." Rhyme threw down the plans.

Zambelli crossed himself.

"Look here, *Signore* Zambelli," Rhyme said in a dogged voice. "Even with step sections that drop off, you're not going to get very far. I don't need mathematics to know that. I can see just in looking at the plans."

Zambelli groaned. Rhyme slapped the table, making the charts coil. "This is a great engine. I like this engine. The fuel is wonderful, with the oxidizer mixed in, but, one, there's not enough of it, and, two, you can't control the burning."

Zambelli regarded him with mournful eyes. "Yes, is true. She go boom real quick."

"Exactly. Now, what I'm proposing, is to use one of my sorcerous engines to do a number of things. One, to control the fuel burning so that you don't go boom. Two, to increase fuel efficiency by a factor of about ten, so you don't need those step sections. Three, to increase the thrust by a factor of about five. With a full load, the assisted engine will burn for hours and hours. And at the speeds we'll attain, the rocket will get you anywhere."

"Even the moon?"

"Even the moon, for all I know, though I don't know a lot about that sort of thing."

"I do," Zambelli said. "I study orbit mathematics. If the engine burn for five minutes, I fly up into orbit around the earth, then fire again and fly to the moon. Then, I can land on the moon, and fly back. Is wonderful. So, it can be done, with the magic?"

"As I said, this honey will take you anywhere. All you have to do is refill the tanks with water for the return trip." Rhyme pulled at his beard. "Do you know if there's water on the moon?"

Zambelli lifted his head. "Water?"

"Yes. The sorcerous engine runs on steam. You can't run a magic engine on magic. It's a closed loop. Won't work. It takes energy from outside the system, and plenty of it. As long as you have steam power to move the engine parts, you get magic out of it. The moment you lose steam, the magic stops. So, you have to be careful you don't run out of water. Is there water on the moon, in case you run low?"

"Yes! There is water, in the *mare*. The seas on the moon."

"Well, good. There you are. With this one-step rocket you can forget about dropping off pieces along the way. In fact, this design will make a dandy artillery rocket, and that will please Tarlenheim. Now, if we move the whole operation into a dwarfhold, using your plans for the prototype, heavily adapted, we can have the thing ready for a test flight within a few months. That's if we can cannibalize the components that should arrive today. I'll have to look them over before deciding."

Zambelli's face glowed. "You mean . . . it can be done?"

"These plans are pretty good, actually," Rhyme said. "Very imaginative, very advanced thinking. Kind of impractical in spots, but basically workable. What you need is dwarf ingenuity and dwarf engineering. We can do it, for sure."

Zambelli leaped out of his chair and hugged the diminutive engineer, then picked him up like a baby.

Kicking his stubby legs, Rhyme struggled to get free. "Put me down, you big piece of linguine!"

Zambelli planted a wet kiss on the dwarf's cheek and set him down.

Rhyme scrubbed his cheek, scowling. "Don't ever do that again."

"I'm sorry," Zambelli said, beaming. "I'm so happy We going to make history, you and me."

"Just pray the damned contraption doesn't blow up in our faces. By the way, there's another thing you need."

"Yes?"

"My benchtop analytical, a small Babbage calculator. Swiss clockwork to time the engine blasts is fine, but with the whole works linked to my analytical, you'll get more precision, and the sequences can be planned. Also, navigation and astronomical stuff will be much easier."

"Of course," Zambelli said. "It is good that you have made this thing, this small Babbage."

"Damn right. Trouble is, certain other people feel the same way, and are out to get it."

Zambelli crossed himself again. "The devils."

"I guess that's who's behind it. The Unseelie. They want it for the Prussians. We can't let them get it. Once I move my stuff to the dwarfhold, it'll be safe enough. But . . . well . . . I've taken other precautions."

"*Magnifico! Bene.* You are maybe still hungry? More sausage, eh?"

Rhyme's bushy brows rose. "And beer?"

"Ah, *birra!* Of course. All you want. I have more barrels coming today, with the other stuff. Come, let's eat, drink . . ."

Grinning at each other, they headed for the dining room.

CHAPTER 12

TUT, TUT

London bustled with activity, Piccadilly Circus rotating like a merry-go-round. But Olam and van Helsing did not linger in the city. By taking a train from Paddington Station out into the English countryside, they reached Hampshire, about five miles on the far side of Winchester. From the train stop, they enjoyed a leisurely phaeton ride out to Beechtree Court, the country estate of Lord Ashton Montague. The road ran through a stately carpet of foliage and field, with little red, gray-roofed farmsteads in neat patches.

Footmen met the cab to take the luggage while the butler greeted the guests, stating that tea was about to be served on the lawn.

"I'll take that," van Helsing said to one of the men removing luggage from the cab.

"Right you are, guv."

The footman handed over a long, slender object wrapped in brown paper and tied here and there with string. It appeared to be a pole or rod.

"What do you have there?" Tom asked.

"The artifact Montague was interested in." Van Helsing seemed reluctant to say more and Tom didn't press him.

They strolled toward Beechtree Court, a white Georgian manor that sprawled over an acre, nestled among copper beeches and other well-bred trees. Spacious grounds abounded, ending in woods on three sides. To the west, a field sloped down to Southampton high road, which made a graceful curve past the entrance to the manor.

Tom and van Helsing ambled around the east wing, admiring the shrubbery en passant, until finally they came to the back lawn, on which a number of tents had been set up. People stood about in groups of four or five, holding teacups and talking. The guests weren't all human. One dragon, wings folded neatly, forelimbs daintily holding cup and saucer, rounded out the guest list.

A tall, rangy young man wearing a tweed suit approached them. On a babyishly handsome, pug-nosed face he wore a cheery smile, and his manner exuded a breezy bonhomie. "What ho! More guests. Well, the more the jolly well merrier, I always say. Hello, Brewster's the name. Wyndham Brewster, though my *intimes* call me Wynnie. And you are . . . ?"

"Bond," Tom said. "Thomas Bond. And this is my colleague, Dr. Abraham van Helsing of the Sorbonne. We are both postdoctoral students."

"Ah, yes, I saw the guest list. What sort of doctoring do you two fellows do?"

"History," Tom said.

"I have a degree in medicine, but I don't practice, at the moment," van Helsing said.

"What's that long skinny thing you're carrying, Doctor?"

"An historical artifact for Lord Montague."

"He's a bug on history, that's a fact. Splendid. History and medicine, well, there's a strange pairing, but I'll wager a *dashed* interesting one."

"Dashed, yes," Tom said, looking around.

"You're American," Brewster said.

"Yes."

"Thought I detected a twang that could only come from one of our American cousins. I've been to New York once. Had a smashing time, I must say. You look a tad familiar. Have we—?"

"Say," Tom interrupted, "is Lord Ashton Montague around?"

"The old boy's lurking about somewhere, in the shadows probably. He's an eerie old banshee, sometimes, and I say that with great fondness, of course, his being my uncle and all. Uncle by marriage, that is."

"What do you mean by 'banshee' . . . uh—?"

"Just call me Brewster. What do I mean? Oh, he's a moody sort, nose forever in a book, tending to contemplative reveries and brown studies, that sort of thing. A well-read man, and an intelligent one, to be sure. But a trifle, well, withdrawn. Aloof."

"I see. He must have a well-stocked library. Know where it is?"

"East wing, I do believe," Brewster said, taking out of his jacket a polished silver cigarette case. "Yes that's right. East wing, first floor. Lots of shivery things in there, don't you know. Egypt stuff. Mummies and all that moldy lot. Have a cigarette?"

"No, thank you." Van Helsing's interest was suddenly piqued. "He has actual mummies?"

"Well, there are a number of big cases lying about. Truth to tell, I've never paid them much attention, and as far as my ever cracking one open goes, why, I'd as lief dig up a grave, which the act would amount to anyway. They are ever so attractively decorated, though, all these little squiggly symbols and things and stick men with their feet going odd ways and arms sticking out, like so."

Brewster crooked both arms and held them out in a burlesque of Egyptian iconography. "First-rate stuff, if you like that sort of thing."

"Interesting," was van Helsing's comment.

"I think . . . well, I really should get washed up," Tom said.

"Loo's on the second floor, Bond. See Henderson, the butler. Do run along, I'll chat up the good doctor, here."

"Great. I'll see you later, Dr. van Helsing."

"Be careful," van Helsing silently mouthed as he walked away with Wyndham Brewster.

Tom edged past two groups of people, drawing some stares as he passed. He could never predict his being recognized. In this day of primitive photography and image reproduction, people might or might not recognize him from the steel engravings of his likeness in the newspapers.

His part in the battle of Königseig in 1886 had afforded him some notoriety. And it was generally known that he was not of this world, that he had been magicked here by Faerie spells. Spellnapped. Stories about him were told to kids at bedtime all over Europe. He often thought how strange it was to be a secret agent under these circumstances. Ah, well. Nevertheless, he still had some anonymity. A mild disguise was all it took to fool most people.

Yet he could never be really sure.

The back of the house was the conservatory, and its big doors were wide open. He walked in, crossed the length of the plant-cluttered room, through a swinging door, and into the main hall that divided the house. He passed the kitchen without looking in. A guest would hardly be nosing about the help. After passing a ballroom and a salon, he came to the main staircase, leading up to the family's part of the house.

Was there a family? Tom didn't know. Brewster had said he was related by marriage, so there was a wife, presumably, a Lady Montague. She was nowhere in sight. Probably in the backyard having tea with her guests. Not another soul was in sight, in fact. Everyone was out back.

So far, so good. The library? Ah, there, that door, perhaps.

He tiptoed over old, rattling parquet floors, stopped at the door, checked about, and turned the doorknob. Not locked. He cracked the door and peeked in. He neither saw nor heard anyone inside, so he slipped in.

A magnificent library. Walls of books, beautiful books, with bindings of leather, mostly.

Quiet.

He wandered around, peering at hieroglyphs, reading ribbed book spines, contemplating art objects. There were several genuine pieces of Egyptian statuary, one a massive seated pharaoh in dolomite marble. Other artifacts abounded: slate palettes, clay urns, carved wood figures, inlaid boxes, jewelry in cases, hundreds of other curios. And the mummy cases. This was an age during which the looting of Egypt was in full swing.

With some difficulty, Tom tore himself away from the Egyptiana, all of which was extremely interesting, but, after all, he was not here to steal museum pieces. He was here to find a book on rockets, or better yet, plans for rocket engines.

He could see nothing of interest. After a quick search doubts began to rise in his mind. Why go to all this trouble? So what if the Secret Service got hold of detailed plans? What then? Well, they'd know more about the rocket's range and other capabilities, and the threat would be better assessed.

Okay, as long as the purpose was clear in his mind. But something nagged at him. He didn't feel as if he was doing enough. Good to know about a threat, better—best!—to eliminate it entirely. What he wanted to do, he couldn't do, which was to take the *Wagner* out and attack the von Bremen compound and bomb the living crap out of it.

But that would be wrong.

Sigh.

No, not wrong, though it would be an act of naked aggression. "Preemptive strike," was the euphemism. Well, sometimes such were justified. He wondered if the Second Compact nations, France, Britain, and the others, would sit still for it.

The library door opened and in walked Lord Ashton Montague. Tom recognized him from Secret Service file engravings.

"Greetings," Montague said pleasantly.

"Good evening, Lord Montague," Tom said casually. "I took the liberty of examining your Egyptian collection. The door wasn't locked. I do hope you don't mind."

Montague was a tall man, dark of hair and eye. He had a foreign look about him, something Levantine, perhaps. His skin was almost olive. His voice was unquestionably English, though.

"Not at all. Have we met?"

"I'm presuming on your hospitality, I'm afraid. I came with Dr. van Helsing. I'm a fellow student. Thomas Bond."

"Excellent, Mr. Bond. Then you're quite welcome. Does Egypt happen to be your field?"

"Uh, no. Recent history, contemporary European studies, that sort of thing. But Egypt has always been an interest."

"Then you might find this singular. Do you see this figure, the hippopotamus? Pre-dynastic, possibly the earliest example of faïence known."

"Glaze," Tom said.

"Yes. You do know a bit. This object is over five thousand years old. Isn't that marvelous?"

"Surely. This is a fine headdress. Some princess's, I take it?"

"Oh yes. New Kingdom. We don't know what noble head wore it, but surely she was a fine lady. Lapis lazuli, dark serpentine, red carnelian, inlaid with gold. Exquisite."

"Absolutely."

"I often daydream about her," Montauge sighed.

"Her? Oh, the princess."

"Yes. She could have been Nefertiti, herself. Queen to Akhnaten, the great apostate."

"Yes," Tom said. "Was he the one who abandoned the worship of Amen-Ra and started a new cult, centering on the sun-god Aten?"

"Yes. He also abandoned Egypt."

"How so?"

"He drew back his armies from Asia and did nothing while bedouin hordes overran Lower Egypt. He was a pacifist. A very ineffectual leader. Egypt would have ceased to exist under his new religion."

"You don't say. May I ask about this pin on your lapel?"

"It is the ankh, the symbol of eternal life. Have you ever heard of the Mystic Lodge of the Temple of Ra?"

"Why, as a matter of fact, yes. Are you a member?"

"Oh, yes. It is an ancient order, representing a tradition of worship that goes back millennia. The ancient gods of Egypt. Would you care for a drink, Thomas? May I call you Thomas?"

"Certainly."

"I'm having one, myself." Montague held up a whiskey bottle.

"What say you?"

I've seen this movie, Tom thought. What makes movie heroes take that drugged drink? You know it's got a Mickey Finn in it. Or poison, or something. Why drink it? Why make it easy for the villain?

"Tell you the truth, my lord, I'm a total abstainer."

"Commendable. Me, I can't resist the grape."

Montague poured himself a generous amount of whiskey, and spritzed a dash of soda into it.

"You also believe in reincarnation," Tom went on.

"Yes. Some of us. I don't put much stock in the notion. In most matters, I tend to be a rationalist. I'm a businessman, an engineer."

"Yes. You make very good steam engines."

"The best. If I do say so, myself."

"They're used all over the world," Tom said. "All over Europa, especially. I believe that most—just as a for instance—most Prussian locomotives run on your engines."

"Not all, certainly. I do have competition in Prussia. And everywhere. Contrary to popular opinion, it is virtually impossible to hold a monopoly for long. Industrial thieves are as common as pickpockets. Commoner. Patents can't always protect you. You need the help of a strong government. To pass laws, to impose tariffs, to give you exclusive license to trade. Being the best at what you do isn't enough. You need the protection of the state."

"So I've heard."

Montague took one swallow of his drink and set it down. "Did you ever see a mummy? Close up?"

Tom turned to the mummy case behind him. "Well, as a matter of fact . . ."

"This one dates from the Middle Kingdom. It's quite a find, really. I headed up the expedition, myself, many years ago. We dug under the ruined pyramid near Saqqara. Found the tomb of . . . no, not the pharaoh for whom the structure was built, but possibly one of his high officials. The casket says his name was Hashamose. I call him Hash for short. Take a look. Sure about that drink?"

Tom stepped up to the casket. "Quite sure, thank you."

With both hands, Lord Montague lifted the heavy wooden lid of the mummy case.

Inside was the usual corpse swaddled in endless bandages.

"There he is. He has slept through four hundred centuries."

"Terrible when you miss a wake-up call."

"Eh? Notice that the body is more than a skeleton. Much of the flesh remains. You see? Feel the mass. Don't be afraid. Substantial, eh? This is a body, not a leather sack full of bones."

"Remarkable." An almost overpowering stench of decay hit Tom's nostrils. It was the odor of rot and fungus and the dust of centuries.

"Quite so, quite so. And now . . . Hash, will you seize our friend?"

The mummy struck like a snake. No sleeper, this one. In a second the undead creature had both bandage-wrapped hands around Tom's throat and was squeezing. Tom thrashed and struggled but could not get free. He reached over the case, snagged a clay pot, and smashed it over the mummy's head. The eyes, cold dark eyes with endless inhuman depths, registered pain, but the strength of the grip increased.

Writhing and struggling, Tom fought with the thing, trying to tear the cold, dead hands away. None of his standard defensive moves seemed to work. The creature was unnaturally strong.

Montague was watching, clinically, almost detached.

"You go down hard, Mr. Bond. Or should I say, Mr. Olam."

Tom croaked an obscenity, but it died in his throat.

"Good night, Mr. Olam," Lord Montague said.

CHAPTER 13

ARISE, FALKENSTEIN

A vast moving endeavor began at Castle Falkenstein. The tons of rocket stuff that had been shipped up from Italy (at great expense), the Zambellis, Rhyme and his tools and appurtenances, Morrolan, Tarlenheim, Marianne along with part of her wardrobe, and bringing up the rear, some Secret Service staffers were all moving to the dwarfhold of Kazak Corom, located in a cavern inside a mountain high in the Alps.

Carting everything and everybody up to the dwarfhold by wagon was unthinkable for many reasons, not the least of which was the Wild Hunt, bands of renegade Faerie who delighted in preying on travelers in the mountains. So it was decided to do the entire move by air, using Bayern's fleet of aeronavy ships.

It was a massive logistics problem, and Tarlenheim set his military mind to solving it. Burning all his candles to nubs the night before the move, he stayed up scribbling on scratch sheets, figuring out the most efficient way to do it, coming to the conclusion that it would take no less than six aerobattleships making no less than eighteen flights. He couldn't believe the amount of stuff Zambelli had shipped. (He cringed at the thought of the bill.)

More thorny was the political problem. Messages by carrier pigeon fluttered back and forth between Kazak Corom and Falkenstein for days. A basic alliance with the hold against the Unseelie and Bismarck had already been forged. Rhyme, under duress, had been the catalyst, his reluctance having to do with the indelicate fact that he had impregnated the daughter of Kazak Corom's Dwarf King. This made negotiations rather difficult. But the alliance had been sealed, and the dwarf engineers of Kazak Corom had developed the technologies used in Bayern's aeronavy fleet thereby saving the day against the Prussians at the battle of Königseig.

The day of the great exodus broke with an almost Biblical piquancy—Marianne half-expected the hoot of a ram's horn and a great shout of "Arise, O Israel!" to go up. The aeroships arrived, and the loading went smoothly.

So did the entire move, for the most part. The aeroships floated up into the Alps and alighted on a ledge where two great iron doors were set into the barren rock of the mountain peak. The doors swung open on massive gimbals, and hundreds of dwarfen stevedores poured out to unload the ships and welcome their human guests.

Kazak Corom was a typical dwarfhold, it was a miniature underground industrial complex. The rock of its cavern floor crawled with railways on which small steam trains chugged to and fro with their loads of metal ore and coal. Factory interiors abounded, crowded with workbenches and machinery: lathes, dies, stamps, and drills. Great cranes hung overhead. Everywhere was industrial activity: smelting, fabricating, forging, hammering, clanging, banging, and riveting. The din was constant and sometimes ear-splitting.

There were residence areas, of course, with ample room for the humans. The Zambellis were quartered a few doors down from Marianne's digs. She found her room charming in a typically dwarfen way. The furniture was tiny, doll-like. Unfortunately, so was the bed. She asked for a bigger one and was told that one would have to be built.

Exhausted, Marianne decided to postpone unpacking. She could hang up her clothes tomorrow. She stripped naked and crawled into what could only be a toddler's starter bed. Well, it was cute. The whole room was cute. She curled up and sighed.

Cute.

Something was stirring in the darkness. At first the noise was a slithering, a sliding, rubbing hiss that came from the far wall. Marianne awoke but did not move. She lay listening as her hand slowly slid under the pillow. Then, like a wound-up spring letting loose, she leaped out of bed, pistol in hand, and pulled her sword out of its bedpost-slung scabbard.

A giant snake's head rose over the carved footboard. The eyes glowed red-hot. The thing's body trailed along the floor, meters of it, coiled, all over the floorboards, its farthest end . . .

. . . coming out of the magic mirror, which Marianne had leaned against the wall near the door.

What was this monster?

A *basilisk*, her knowledge of Faerie lore told her, whose glance can kill.

Avoiding looing into its eyes, she took a swipe at the head. It coiled back, a pink forked tongue slithering out and back like lightning.

Marianne slashed again and again, but the creature was quick. No sluggish python, this. It reared back and struck, and Marianne had to throw herself against the wall to miss being skewered by fangs as long as human fingers. More snake body was spilling through the mirror, wriggling out like ointment from a tube, and when she bounced off the dwarfenly cute armoire and fell amongst the slithering length of it on the floor, she found that it was disgustingly wet and slimy, not dry like real snakeskin.

She leaped to her feet, tripped, and crawled to the mirror, where, on her feet again, she brought her saber down hard, cutting halfway through the snake on the first try, hacking at it until it was completely severed. The end inside the room commenced to rear up and dance and twitch, spraying foul-smelling liquid all over.

Marianne let out a scream of revulsion and began hacking blindly at anything that moved. The entire room became one writhing, wriggling, slimy mass, coils within coils, slippery, quivering, and wet, and she decided she'd had enough. Lurching for the door, she slipped and fell on her buttocks, and the snake mass enveloped her, laving her naked body with its hideous wetness, curling itself around her torso and in between her legs, obscenely prodding and probing. And then it began squeezing. A wet vise closed in on her.

Marianne began to lose consciousness, the life flowing out of her like juice from a winepress.

"Help," she tried to yell, but couldn't quite manage it.

Eyes regarded her. Small eyes. Goblin eyes.

Goblins? Rather superfluous, she decided as the darkness deepened.

Unconsciousness closed in.

And then something happened. A great snarling went up, paired with the skittering of claw and talon, the ripping and tearing of flesh, the din of a conflict between creatures of the night. A demoniac howling commenced and continued for some time. Along with this, there came the pattering of dozens of small feet running in panic and the babble of demonic voices, retreating into faintness . . . until quiet finally descended.

Marianne came to her senses. She was lying on her stomach on the floor. She raised her head, turned over, and saw Morrolan, the wizard, standing by the door, smiling impishly at her.

She gave a yelp of indignation. Grinning, he threw her his cloak. She gathered it up, wrapped it around herself, and rose.

"Sorry," Morrolan said, "I have to admit I was enjoying the sight. Most ungentlemanly of me. But you looked rather comic. Forgive me."

"I forgive you. I have half a mind to let you look all you like—if you were the one who saved my life."

"I am he, my dear."

Marianne looked down. "The mirror."

Morrolan chuckled. "A Trojan horse. Someone should have tumbled to it, but Rhyme is a damned laconic bugger. He really should have told someone."

"He told me. It's my fault. I never guessed that it could be a doorway."

"It can, with the proper spells."

Marianne looked about. The room was a shambles, but the floors were completely dry. "What did you do? What happened to the basilisk?"

"Gone. It was an ectoplasmic manifestation, anyway. Fully capable of doing you to death, but not a material presence."

"What did you set upon it?"

"A mongoose. A transmogrified one, to be sure."

"And . . . were there goblins here?"

"Oh, yes. They sodded off when the ruckus began. The basilisk was the assault force, the goblins followed, probably with the purpose of stealing something."

"What, I wonder?"

"Something of Rhyme's. They assumed the mirror was still in Rhyme's workshop."

"Oh, of course. I'll break the thing immediately."

"No need," Morrolan said. "I've sealed it with a protection

spell." He stooped and picked the mirror up. "Let me take it off your hands. I've a feeling it could come in handy."

"You're welcome to it."

"Well, good night." Morrolan opened the door. Outside were crowds of dwarfs, along with the Zambellis, Tarlenheim, and almost, it seemed, everyone else in the dwarfhold.

"It's all over," Morrolan announced.

Grumbling, everyone milled off to bed.

Still holding the door open, Morrolan asked, "Mean what you said about letting me look all I want?"

"Good night, Morrolan," Marianne said firmly, but with a sly half smile.

"Good night, Marianne."

"And thank you very much."

"For what?" Morrolan said with a shrug.

Still half-grinning, Marianne let him leave without an answer.

CHAPTER 14

THE TEMPLE OF RA

Tom Olam woke up and found that he was strapped to a table. It was in an odd room. Looked like a church, sort of. Actually, it looked like something out of a movie. It was decorated like an Egyptian tomb, walls covered in hiero-glyphics and frescoed with scenes of animal-headed gods, buxom cow-goddesses, pharaohs and queens and courtiers and slaves, and a hundred other figures. Against the far wall stood what appeared to be an altar, a jackal-headed god in a niche standing over it. Braziers smoldered throughout the room, and candles flickered on the altar and on various shrines flanking it.

Never liked church much, Tom thought.

Well, he had dodged the old Mickey Finn in the drink bit, only to fall for the old zombie-mummy-in-the-mummy-case bit.

Tom sighed. What was this business with the table? He craned his head. He was naked, except for a few preliminary wrappings of cloth, here and there.

Various vials and urns occupied tables to the side. Nearby, a brazier on a tripod heated up a clay pot bubbling with something.

A section of stone wall swung out, and in walked a robed Montague, accompanied by two mummies, Hash and a buddy, whoever he was.

Montague approached the altar, held out both arms, and prayed: "O great Anubis, lord of the underworld, thy servants beseech thee. Direct our feet along the way, show us the light, guide us to everlasting life, so that we may serve thee throughout eternity and do thy bidding. Whatsoever is thy wish, it shall be our command."

Montague bowed and withdrew from the altar. He walked toward the table.

"I see you're up," he commented, stopping to stir the pot over the brazier.

"An elixir brewed of nine tanna leaves?" Tom ventured.

Montague raised his dark brows. "You are strangely knowledgeable, Mr. Olam. This is a secret known only to a chosen few. How came you by such knowledge?"

"I stay up nights reading."

Montague smiled. "I admire your sangfroid, my friend." He moved to the table. "I assume you get the general idea here."

"Sure. You're going to teach me how to do the world's best Lon Chaney impression."

"I have no idea who or what you're referring to. You are a very strange young man. But I'll take that answer as a yes. I am about to give you the gift of eternal life. You will live and walk the earth forever. But only at my command, and only if I give you the elixir of life. I need more help around the house, so I'm hiring you as a servant. No pay, just room and board. Or should I say, crypt and a cup of tea now and then. Unless . . ."

"Unless."

"Unless you tell me all I want to know about the Bavarian rocket program."

"I don't get cable."

Montague regarded him somberly for a moment, then shrugged. "Very well. Hashamose, hand me that blade."

Tom asked, "You need a knife for what?"

"Well, you see, in order for you to become a mummy, you have to die first."

"Naturally."

"Are you sure you can't tell me something?"

"I can tell you where Tutankhamen's tomb is."

Montague chuckled. "I know where it is. I buried him. In fact, I killed the whelp. The boy was backsliding, fearing his father's vengeful ghost. He had to be eliminated."

"I see. How old are you, anyway?"

"Five millennia, give or take a hundred years. I don't celebrate birthdays."

"How did you get started in the mummy business?"

"It's a long story."

"I've got time."

"Yes, you do, Mr. Olam. You have all of eternity."

The wall swung open again, and in walked van Helsing, brandishing a long wooden staff. He was followed by a nervous Wyndham Brewster.

"I say, what the devil is all this?" Brewster said, eyes goggling. Astounded, he took in the room.

"Van Helsing!" Montague said. "You brought the Levite staff. To use against me, no doubt."

"If necessary," van Helsing said.

Both mummies lurched toward van Helsing. He kept them at bay with the staff. They would not venture within its reach.

"Brewster, cut Mr. Olam loose," van Helsing said.

"What's all this, then, Uncle Ash?" Brewster said as he picked up the knife and began to cut Tom free of his bonds.

"Wynnie, do shut up," Montague said wearily. "Cut the man free and then go. By the way, you're never to darken my door again."

"I shall do no door-darkening round these purlieus, that I can assure you, avuncular one. Walking mummies, heathen idols, tsk tsk. Nasty business, eh what? I say, Olam, you're stark naked. Just what in heaven's name did you intend to do to this man, Uncle of mine? If you don't mind my saying so, this whole business is taking on a sinister aspect."

"I wouldn't mind a thing, Wynnie, if you'd only shut your trap. You bloody idiot."

Brewster bristled. "Look here, I'm quite aware that you and I don't see gimlet to gimlet, but that doesn't call for personal invective."

Tom jumped off the table and spotted his clothes lying in a pile in the corner. He grabbed them and ran for the door.

"Brewster, let's go!"

"Be right with you, Olam. Now see here, Uncle, I've had my eye on you ever since you married Aunt Daphne, and don't think I didn't have an inkling as to what shenanigans were going on at Beechtree Court all along, though I didn't *quite* know the extent of it. I've checked into your background, sir, and, well, not to put too fine a point on it, you're a bit of a fraud. Your peerage was granted not ten years ago. You're a . . . well, I'll flat out say it. You're a social climber."

Ashton Montague clutched at his chest in mock pain, as if mortally wounded. "Run along, Wynnie, you dim bulb. Don't be surprised if Hashamose, here, pays you a visit some night."

"Does he play billiards?"

"Brewster, time to skedaddle!" Tom was by this time completely dressed.

"Right-o," Brewster said.

Montague said, "You had better get out while the magic in that staff is still efficacious. It won't last all night. Not here in the temple of the old gods."

"He's right," van Helsing said, still fending off the two mummies.

The three men left, slamming the wall shut after them. Van Helsing and Brewster led Tom back the way they had come, down a narrow passage and up crooked stairs. At the top was an opening, a library bookshelf swung out from the wall.

All three men pushed the bookshelf back into place, and then slid a large sofa in front of it.

"Well, that will hold them for a bit," Brewster said.

"There must be another exit. We had better leave immediately," van Helsing said. "This staff is weakening. I am no magician, but even I feel it."

Tom asked, as they were leaving, "What is that thing?"

"The staff of an ancient Levite priest."

"I say, would you fellows be at all interested in coming over to my place?"

"Capital idea, old boy," Tom said.

"Splendid. My automotive's right out front."

The house proper was still mostly empty. As the men walked out into the hall, party noises came from the conservatory.

"Montague's neglecting his guests," Tom said. "Tell me, Dr. van Helsing, how old is that staff?"

"I have only a general idea. It dates back at least to the Babylonian exile. Possibly further. Hebrew magic is traditionally efficacious in Egypt."

"Are you saying that staff belonged to . . . ?"

"Aaron? I make no such claim. I can reliably trace its provenance to an Israelite scholar in Mesopotamia in the sixth century B.C. Beyond that is mere conjecture."

Wynnie Brewster's automotive was a sporty little roadster of green-painted steel with brass fittings, typically British in design, from its red leather seats to the strap across its bonnet.

"Won't be long," Wynnie said. "It's got a dry-cell boiler warmer and I left it on. Let me fire up, and we'll pop off in half a jif."

The boiler came up to steam in less than a minute. There was room on the single seat for a driver and one passenger, but it was broad enough to accommodate two with squeezing.

"Tom!" van Helsing said with just a little alarm. "What about your rocketry books?"

"At this point getting back to Bayern is my top priority," Tom said.

Brewster engaged the clutch and shot down the driveway, then swung out onto the high road, turning left without so much as a glance in either direction. Thereafter he drove with an aristocratic attitude toward road ownership, claiming the lion's share of it, beeping indignantly when oncoming traffic challenged his birthright, one hand jauntily on the wheel, the other arm crooked over the door, declaiming at the top of his lungs about anything and everything all the way.

Tom and van Helsing learned much about the countryside, its populace, its recreational opportunities (mostly what animals there were to shoot at), its social structure (who gives the best parties), and its general rating in terms of the good life (quite high, in fact).

In less than an hour they arrived at Brewster Hall, a modest manor house with a classical front in wood and a rough stone veneer.

"We'll be roughing it a bit," Brewster said. "My man's off visiting his mum in Croydon."

"His name wouldn't be Jeeves, would it?" Tom asked.

Brewster gave him an odd look. "Jeeves? Why on earth would you ask that, old bean? Jeeves. What a singularly odd name. No, matter of fact, the chappie's name is Slope. Obadiah Slope. I suppose that's an odd name, too, in a way. But there you are. And here we are."

Brewster Hall was given over to a man's man's version of country living: guns on the wall, tiger-skin rug before the fireplace, red leather easy chairs, well-stocked bar, cigar humidors, pewter ashtrays, pewter drinking mugs (lots of pewter about), oak furniture, pipe racks. The curtains were functional, most of the rugs a bit threadbare, and very little art showed itself. The odor of aromatic coarse-cut pipe tobacco pervaded the Hall.

Tom like the place.

"I say, would you fellows care for a nightcap?"

"Sure," Tom said. "Would you happen to know when the last train leaves for London this evening?"

"I'm afraid you've missed it, *mon vieux*. No matter. First thing after breakfast—though Slope isn't here to fry any breakfast up, and I don't quite know what to do about that, but we'll think of something—I'll give you a lift to the station, and Bob's your uncle."

"Thanks. I wonder if there's any possibility of our getting back to London tonight. At least, speaking for myself. I don't know about the good doctor here."

Van Helsing shrugged. "I, myself, have no reason to get back any sooner than tomorrow morning."

"I say, Olam, old chap, it would be rather a hardship to get you back tonight. Oh, I'd drive you myself and not care a ha'penny, were it not that I'm fagged out. Got up at six this morning to go potting at some grouse. Didn't hit a thing, but it does sap the strength, all that walking and potting."

There came a loud knock on the door.

"Gadzooks, who could that be this time of night?"

"Brewster, we'll be in the study. Rather, we won't be in the study. Clear?"

"Clear as a glass ice cube, old bean. Mum's the word."

After the two men hid, Brewster answered his front door.

"Ah, Mr. Brewster. Good evening. Your man's off tonight, is he?"

"Inspector Motherwell! Yes, Slope's flown the coop. Well, what brings you calling at this ungodly hour? Not that you're unwelcome anytime at *chez* Brewster."

Motherwell, a compact, red-faced man, took out his pocket watch. "Why, it's not half past ten, Mr. Brewster."

"Oh. Well, hate to be abrupt, Motherwell, but as you can see my man's away and it's been catch-as-catch-can for two days. What is it you want, then?"

"We're looking for a man who was at your uncle's place tonight. Thomas Olam is his name. We've been requested by Scotland Yard to take him into custody."

"Indeed. What's he done?"

"Well, he's done nothing that I know of, but he is possibly an agent of a foreign government who's entered the country without registering as such. The London chaps want a talk with him, is all."

"I see. Well, if I see this agent fellow running about, I'll be sure to ring you up. Now, if that's all . . ."

"Uh, sir, you were seen driving off with them in your motor vehicle this evening. Olam and another man, another foreigner."

"Eh? Well . . . why . . . uh, yes, that's quite true. No disputing that datum, not one iota. Quite the truth, yes. But you see, I drove them both into Winchester, and . . ."

Motherwell looked at his watch again. "Winchester. You left Montague's not an hour ago. I just missed you. And you're back already?"

"Might as well own up to it, Motherwell, I've been speeding again. Clap me in irons and knock up the magistrate, you have your man."

"I suppose I couldn't come in and take a look, myself?"

"Motherwell, do you mean to say that you doubt my word?"

"Not a bit, Mr. Brewster. Though I might be back with a warrant."

"Then you're in like a shot, Inspector, but not until you have that warrant in your grubby little German hand. You do understand?"

"Perfectly, sir. Perfectly. Well within your rights. I'll be saying good evening to you, Mr. Brewster."

"I'll be saying ditto, Motherwell. Do stop back."

Brewster watched the policeman get back into his automotive and drive off, before closing the door and walking to the study.

"He's popped off. Come out for that drink, men. Seems you're in a spot of trouble, Olam."

"I quite agree," Tom said. "Very sporting, what you did, Brewster."

"Tosh, think nothing of it. Though I'm hanged about what I'll do if Motherwell makes it back with that slip of legal paper."

"I'll take to the open country. Dr. van Helsing, I see no reason why you can't stay here for the night. You're not in the soup, as far as I know."

"Thomas, I can't help but feel that our fates are inextricably entwined, at least for the immediate future."

"You may be right, *Herr Doktor*," Tom said. "It would probably be wise if we assumed they want you as badly as they do me."

"I say, you two are in a considerably bigger pickle than I'd first imagined. Is it really all that bad?"

"Montague is a Steam Lord. Who knows what government organs he has in his pocket, including Scotland Yard."

"You're right about that," Brewster said, leaning against the mantel. "'Midas' Montague is my moniker for him. Not much he can't buy, and not many he can't buy off. But see here, old bean, I can't let you go traipsing off over bog and fen at the dark of the moon. I'll drive you anywhere."

"Big risk," Tom said. "If we're caught, you'll be in the soup with us."

"I'm already hip-deep in the muligatawny, *mon vieux*, at least vis-à-vis my dear uncle, what with his bandaged bunkies threatening to drop round for tea."

"Then you will need this," van Helsing said, proffering the Levite staff.

"Thanks awfully, Dr. Van. Just stand it up over there by the Zulu spear."

"Certainly."

Wynnie Brewster's eyes lit up with an epiphanal glow. "Oh, I say."

Tom looked up from his easy chair. "What is it?"

"I have an absolutely *ripping* idea."

"Rip away."

"You want to go into London? We'll take the *Stiffy May!*"

"What's that?"

"My airship! *Stephanie May*, actually."

"You have an airship?"

"Well, it's not a dirigible. It's a balloon-bag type, hot-air variety. A nifty little racer. Has room for three at least in the gondola. I've competed in the Brighton Cup with her a few times. Finished in a dead heat with a crippled pelican, but it was royal fun. Haven't taken her up in donkey's ears—but, well, come round back and I'll show you."

CHAPTER 15

WYNNIE-THE-FOOL

Brewster's private blimp (which is what Tom would have called it in another place and time) lived in an ancient barn in the back of the house. The tinplate gondola and folded hot-air sac rolled out the big doors with minimal effort. Clearing barn junk out of the way first was the real task. Once the contraption was out, though, it became a matter of unfolding the sac a bit and firing up the twin coal-oil-fired boilers, one for driving the propellers, one to provide hot air for lift. In about ten minutes' time the air sac had inflated with superheated vapor and was floating over Brewster Hall like a giant sausage. It dwarfed the tiny gondola, still anchored to the ground.

"Navigating at night is going to be tricky business," Tom said.

"Navigate? You don't navigate a balloon-bag airship, old boy, so much as you jolly well go where the wind has a whim to take you. There's a saucy little zephyr blows down to London at night. I know, I've taken her up at dusk, just to see if . . . well, one never knows when one might want a fast escape, eh?"

"I'm game if you are," Tom said. "Dr. van Helsing?"

"I have always wanted a ride in one of these machines."

"Well, climb aboard, *Herr Doktor*, and I'll take her up straightaway."

And that Wyndham Brewster did, more or less, but not before loading the gondola with victuals, potables, and armaments: a cured ham, a loaf of bread, a tin of pâté de foie gras, a crock of caviar, a box of saltines, six bottles of liquor, a shotgun, three pistols, and two rifles.

Thus provisioned, the *Stephanie May* rose into the dark Hampshire night, its twin propellers chopping at the wind. Although not providing terrific thrust, they did serve to push the craft along merrily.

"I've never flown by instruments," Brewster said, "but here's the compass—says we're traveling southeast, and that's the way to go. Here's the altimeter, and we're rising, sluggishly, but rising. All instruments with radium-salt dials. So, we're bang on course and off to a jolly good start."

"Great," Tom said.

"Brandy, gentlemen? I suspect a night chill will descend forthwith, once we get a little altitude."

"A drink would go well," van Helsing said. "Tom, I think it is about time you told us what this is all about."

"I can't, *Herr Doktor*," Tom said. "Sorry."

"Well, I quite understand," Brewster said. "Hush, hush, and all that cloak and dagger stuff, what?"

"More or less," Tom admitted.

The Hampshire countryside slid past below, a scattering of lights across vast expanses of gloom. Off to the northeast, the city of Winchester glowed, rapidly receding as the *Stephanie May* nosed into a prevailing southerly airstream.

A jagged finger of fire scratched the darkness farther south.

"Bit of dicey weather ahead," Brewster noted.

"Thunderstorm," Tom said. "We'd better put down well before London."

"Excellent idea, that," Wynnie Brewster said. "Easier said than done, though. I've never landed in a populated area before. I think we should float on out near the coast a bit, some links and whatnot there."

"If that storm doesn't drag us out to sea," Tom warned.

"Oh, *Stiffy* won't let us get dragged off. Will you, old girl?" Brewster patted the instrument panel.

"I hope she's up to it," Tom said.

"More brandy?"

"Please."

"Have some caviar."

"Hand me a saltine," van Helsing put in.

They missed London by a wide margin. Whatever was rolling below, it was not that great city. Rain began to pelt the gondola's windows.

"Have an inkling where we are?" Tom asked.

"Not the foggiest, I'm afraid," Wynnie Brewster said, pouring himself the last of the brandy. "You know, old boy, forgive me, but I honestly can't say as I give much of a deuce."

Tom burped. "That pâté is rich stuff."

"Blasted frogs, nailing a poor birdie's foot down and stuffing corn down its gullet. Cruel beyond reason."

"Yeah. How's our altitude?"

"Well, let's give a look-see. I can't read that dial. Can you read that dial? I can't read that dial."

"Dr. van Helsing," Tom said groggily. "Read that dial."

Van Helsing leaned forward and squinted. "We appear to be dropping."

"Blast," Brewster exclaimed.

"Wynnie, the fuel flow control," Tom said. "We have to have more lift."

"Blast it all," Brewster said, more emphatically.

"What blast?" Tom asked.

"Tommy, old fellow, there's been a major cock-up."

"What sort of cock-up, Wynnie, old sport?"

"I've just remembered why I haven't taken old *Stiffy* up lately."

"Oh, no."

"Oh, yes. A leak. Leak in the air sac, old boy. Clean forgot. I knew there was a reason she was sitting out there in the shed, all forlorn." Wynnie thumped the control panel. "Sorry, old girl. I sent you up to bat with a sticky wicket. Well, we'll just do this, then."

Brewster reached under the panel and pulled a lever. The gondola lurched upward.

"What was that?"

Brewster beamed. "I released all the ballast, all in a go."

"Wynnie, you idiot," Tom exclaimed.

"I say, Tommy, what's the fuss?"

"Now we can't land."

Wynnie said, "Don't be silly, Tom, old son, we can just use the exhaust valve on the bag to spill out some hot stuff."

"But if our descent rate is too much we don't have anything to trim us out."

"Oh." Brewster's face fell. "I say, you do have a point."

Tom said, "Look down there, can you see anything?"

Brewster pressed his nose to the Eisenglass window. "I see absobloominglutely damn-all."

"So do I," Tom said. "We've blown out over the sea. We're going to crash in it. We're going into the drink, Wynnie."

"Well, there's only one thing to do, isn't there?"

"What's that, Wynnie?"

"Open another bottle."

The storm erupted into full force. It was a thunderstorm down from the Midlands blowing out to sea, taking the *Stephanie May* with it. Lightning crackled, gales blew, and the little airship spun about in the maelstrom. Rain beat on the windows. The passengers were cozy enough, but the ship continued to drop precipitously.

"We will have to do something at some point," Tom said thickly, slurping brandy. "That burner on maximum?"

"Maxitively, old boy."

"We're still going down," Tom said. "Well, then we have to lighten up if we want to make it to the French coast."

"I suppose," Wynnie said. "We could throw out some of this debris."

Tom kicked the hatch open, and Wynnie threw out two dead bottles, an empty tin, and some paper from the cracker box.

"That wasn't awfully much, was it?" Wynnie said.

Tom agreed. "Not nearly enough."

"What shall we do?"

"Unbolt the propeller engine and boiler and heave it overboard. Have any tools?"

Wynnie opened a compartment under the control panel. It was empty, save for a signal flare. He gave Tom a bleak smile.

Tom reached inside his jacket and got out his Swiss army knife. It was unlike any ever made. He had designed it himself. Van Helsing moved aside and let Tom get to the access panel at the cabin's rear. Tom had the screws out in a jiffy, then folded the panel aside exposing the machinery of the engines. But there was not enough light by which to work.

"What's our altitude?"

"Less than a thousand," van Helsing said.

"Damn. Wynnie, light up that flare."

Wynnie did so after rolling down a window and sticking the thing partway out. The flare sputtered and spat and sparked, but flooded the cabin with enough raw red light by which to work. Tom began unbolting components and handing them over to van Helsing, who pitched them out the door.

"How do you know when to stop?" van Helsing asked.

"I'll take out parts until the thing stops, then I'll put that last part back in."

"Oh. Good plan."

Tom continued unscrewing and unbolting. The small steam engine and heater had an amazing number of parts, and the dismantling was a tough job under these conditions. The gondola rocked and swayed, the rain beat against the cabin windows, and the little ship spun about, all to the tune of lightning and thunder.

"We've stopped our descent," van Helsing announced.

"Good show, lads," Wynnie said.

Suddenly, a sound like a great flapping came from above.

"Oh, damn," Wynnie said.

"We're going down again," van Helsing said.

Tom put away his tool-knife. "That's it, we're done for. That leak just became a tear."

Brewster tossed the flare away. "Olam, van Helsing, I'm awfully sorry. I've gone and gotten us killed."

"Think nothing of it, old boy," Tom reassured him.

"Have a drink," Brewster suggested.

"Don't mind if I do."

Tom took a swig from the bottle. "Wynnie, old bean, you wouldn't happen to have an inflatable life raft?"

"What's that?"

"Inflatable life raft!" Tom suddenly shouted, snapping his fingers.

"Eh?"

"That inflatable life raft was a balloon-parachute! That means that Hauptmann is alive!"

"Good show," Brewster said. "I'm so happy for you. How's our altitude, Dr. van Helsing?"

"We have no altitude," van Helsing said.

The gondola hit the water with a horrific smack, instantly flooding.

"Abandon ship!" Brewster ordered, and the crew obeyed. The gondola sank quickly, but the air sac stayed partially afloat, and the survivors desperately clung to it. But not for long. The hot vapor inside the sac cooled and condensed, and the sac began to sink, dragged down by the water-logged gondola. In a few minutes' time, nothing remained on the surface of the stormy sea but three bobbing men.

"Blast," Wynnie said.

"What?" Tom asked.

"Forgot to save the ham. We'll be famished before long."

"We won't be needing any breakfast, Wynnie. I should have grabbed a gun."

Suddenly, not far away, a bulbous mass of steel plate topped by a windowed tower appeared. A vessel of some sort was rising from the sea. A high, fishlike tail fin jutted from its stern giving it the appearance of an enormous steel shark. The craft resembled no seaworthy vessel on earth.

A hatch in the tower sprang open, and men spilled out onto the deck. They threw lines to the survivors and pulled them in. Then the sailors ushered their guests down through the hatchway.

They descended into a metal compartment crowded with pipes, machinery, and controls, presumably the bridge of the vessel. The hatch above was sealed, and one man shouted orders. Men at the controls pulled levers and threw switches. Deep within the craft, machinery hummed and throbbed.

"We'll go below," one of the sailors told the survivors. "Captain wants to see you after you've dried out. I'll show you to your quarters."

Brewster said, "Sailor, I do hope you don't think me rude and ungrateful, but what in blue blazes is this thing we're on?"

"This is a submersible," the sailor said. "A submarine boat."

"Topping. Who's the skipper?"

"Captain Nemo."

CHAPTER 16

NOW, HERE'S MY PLAN

In a sequestered room of the dwarfhold, Rhyme called the engineering planning meeting to order. Sitting around the enormous table were over half a dozen dwarfs, along with Morrolan, Marianne, Zambelli, and Tarlenheim.

"I've been working all night," Rhyme said, "and I've come to the conclusion that even the revised plan for the rocket won't work."

"What's wrong with it?" Zambelli demanded.

"It's too . . ." Rhyme scowled. "It's too *human*."

"*Ma, che cazzo?*" Zambelli appealed to Marianne. "What's he mean?"

"It's all brute force, all fire and shitstorms, like everything human. The damned thing won't ever get off the ground."

"Sure, she get off the ground, ba-boom, like that!"

"Exactly," Rhyme said sardonically. "Big ba-boom. You shoot this off, and there's no telling where it will end up. There's no real way to steer it, no way to keep it stable in flight, no way . . . very important! . . . no way to *land* the thing without crashing it. Anyone climbing aboard this giant firecracker would be a suicidal fool."

"That's not true!" Zambelli retorted. "He would be a hero!"

"He'd be dead," Rhyme said. "So I've redone the plans and come up with a totally revised design. Pass these around."

The drawings went round the table. When Zambelli got a look at them, his face drained of color. "*Madonna!*"

"Right, I'm using most of my sorcerous engines as a backup in case the rocket engine fails in flight. The levitation engine can provide some lift, but I wouldn't want to depend on it. It's only for use as a last resort. See these deflectors and this system of baffles and tubes? They direct the rocket blast either out the back, for forward thrust, or straight down, for lift. Or a combination of the two. Also, they steer. Really, Zambelli, I'm using your rocket engine, but I'm just redirecting the flow. It's still your engine and fuel."

"Thank you, God," Zambelli said, mopping his brow. "But I see what you do. Is good, is good. She fly like that."

"She'll fly," Rhyme said. "These stubby wings are an attempt at a heavier-than-air flying machine. Well, it almost works, but not quite. You need some of the rocket blast directed downward to stay up in the air. Now, out in space, you can channel all the blast out the rear tubes."

"Sure, sure," Zambelli said.

"And right here, in this section," Rhyme continued, "my new invisibility engine, for stealth."

"Interesting," Tarlenheim said. "I think I like it. It's a big ship."

"The military potential is fairly obvious, but that's not my department," Rhyme said; then, turning to the dwarf contingent, he asked, "Do you think we can build it, Steamfitter?"

The dwarf named Steamfitter shrugged. "Most of it is fairly straightforward. We can build it, Rhyme, as long as you take care of this sorcerous stuff. I see no real problems. And since you're paying good money, I'll guarantee there won't be any."

"How about you, Riveter?"

"We can build the hull," Riveter said. "We can roll the brass sheeting as thin as you want it. Or thinner."

"Not too thin. But not too thick, either. We don't need armor. This ship will be too fast for anyone to hit. Stick to the specifications."

"Neither too thick nor too thin. Check."

"Good. Morrolan, you said you had an idea."

The wizard nodded. "I think I've divined how Marianne's magic mirror really works. I have an idea about adapting it as a communications device. This ship should have some way of communicating with the ground over long distances."

"That's a fine idea," said Tarlenheim. "I hope you succeed."

"As I said, it's an idea. If it works, I think there's a way of adapting it still further. It could be quite spectacular. But I'll know more after I cogitate at some length."

"I'm still worried about Tom," Marianne said. "Is there a way of using the mirror again to contact him?"

"I think so," Morrolan answered. "I think I've just about undone all the spells that were cast on it to do the basilisk trick. I'll recast them after modifications. But I'm fairly sure the mirror's safe to use for a limited amount of time."

"I want to do it as soon as possible," Marianne said. "I'm worried sick."

"We'll try. Come to my room this evening."

Marianne lifted her eyebrows at this but said nothing.

"Don't forget," Tarlenheim said, "if you build it in the hold, you'll need a way of getting it out."

"Easy," Steamfitter said. "The entire top of the mountain opens up. We have to air the place out now and then."

"Really? Remarkable!"

Shaking his head, Zambelli continued to pore over the plans. "I hope she work now."

"It will work," Rhyme said. "I guarantee it. All right, everybody, you all have your assignments. See me later if you're unclear on anything. Now, we get to work. This thing has to be built in record time."

Rising, Tarlenheim said, "I will second that motion most emphatically. The Prussians may already have a complete working weapon to throw at us. We must hit back at them with something that will make them gasp, something that will tell them they are wasting their time. I think this contrivance will do the trick."

Zambelli had been reduced to dyspeptic grumbling. Presently, he threw the plans aside and got to his feet. "I'm hungry. Good-bye."

"I'll need you for consultation on the rocket engine, signore Zambelli," Rhyme said.

Zambelli stopped and gave a sulky look over his shoulder. "Is really true?"

Rhyme nodded, smiling. "Of course. You're a good engineer, Zambelli."

Zambelli's mouth turned slightly upward at the corner. "You're very nice to say that." He seemed mollified.

"I mean it. One good engineer recognizes another." Rhyme grinned. "Besides, I'm famished, too. Have any more of that sage sausage?"

"Plenty," Zambelli said, laughing. "Come, we eat, we drink *la birra*, we talk rockets."

"You know, I kind of like that Italian beer. You wouldn't think Italians made good beer."

CHAPTER 17

DEEP CALLETH
UNTO DEEP

"Captain blooming Nemo," Brewster said, staring into the mirror above the washbasin. The cabin the three men occupied was cramped in the extreme, yet had room enough for three stacked bunks. It could have served as quarters for three junior officers, if there were such aboard this strange craft. After having their wet clothes gathered up for drying and cleaning, the men were given one-piece peacloth coveralls, along with gum-soled shoes.

"I don't believe it," Brewster went on. "I mean, I've read the newspaper accounts, heard all about him, fabled in song and story, and all that rot, but to be actually aboard his dashed submersible, well, never in my wildest dreams, I must say."

"I hear he is a hard man," van Helsing said.

"Be thankful we weren't picked up by the Prussians," Tom said. "At least, I'm thankful."

"What's his country?" Brewster asked. "Nemo's, I mean. What land does he hail from? I don't believe I've ever run across a mention of it."

"No one knows," van Helsing said. "The name itself gives no clue. *Nemo* in Latin means 'no one.'"

"That so? Well, you'd never know by me. *Amo, Amas, Amat* is about all I can muster, and that under duress."

There came a knock at the door. Van Helsing opened it and a bearded man in an officer's uniform, or what looked like one, poked his head in. "The captain will see you now."

"Right. Come, gents, time to meet this man of mystery."

"And a mastermind, if ever there was one," van Helsing said.

They were led through a labyrinth of corridors of steel and brass stuffed with mechanical clutter. Pipes and conduits ran everywhere, as did cables and wiring of every sort. Illumination came from oval panels that glowed with a cold light. Somewhere to the stern of the great vessel beat the heart of some mighty mechanical beast; its powerful rhythms could be felt in the soles of the feet and the cavity of the chest.

The officer swung aside a hatch and gestured the men into the chamber beyond.

The three castaways entered the room and stopped, looking about in awe at a spacious salon of plush velvet, polished brass, and damask. There were settees and other amenities arranged about the room, and a bookcase occupied one corner. A tall, black-haired man in a utilitarian blue uniform stood by an oval bubble of a window set into the far bulkhead; he gazed out into the depths. This was no captain's cabin, no wardroom of a military craft. This was the home of a cultivated man who lived under the sea.

The man turned to greet his guests. "I am Nemo. Who might you be?"

Van Helsing bowed and introduced himself, then introduced his companions.

"Olam," said Nemo. "Of course you were there at the signing of the Second Compact."

"I remember you, Captain Nemo. Glad to be aboard your vessel."

"Frankly, Olam, I think I know why you were at sea in an airship. The Prussian rockets?"

"Well, yes," Tom admitted. "But that's not why I was at sea in this particular airship. Captain, have you been observing anything?"

"I have watched three test firings to date. All three were at least a partial success."

"Did you get close enough to get a look at the actual rockets themselves?"

"We have located the remains of at least one on the sea floor."

"Any chance of recovering some of it?"

"We have already recovered most of it. The device is in pieces, of course. Too many for a spot analysis. The thing hit the water at tremendous speed."

Tom nodded ruefully. "Can I get a look at the debris?"

"Certainly, but my best technicians have already analyzed what they could and have gathered some preliminary data as to its size. It is a tapered cylinder, fashioned of sheet brass, about six meters in length, one meter in diameter, with three rear fins, much like an arrow."

"At that size, its range would be limited," Tom said. "But I have the feeling they are going to push forward with a much bigger rocket very quickly."

"I have that feeling also. These prototypes have performed well. Please, gentlemen, forgive me. Be seated."

All took seats. Nemo then said, "Now, tell me what on earth you were doing out in that storm. Consider yourselves lucky. I, myself, spotted your flare through the periscope only by sheerest happenstance, and then saw the airship crash."

"We're all eternally grateful, Captain Nemo," Wynnie said. "We were escaping from mummies."

Nemo squinted at Wynnie for a moment. "Mummies, you say?"

"Sounds rather recherché, I know. But my uncle, Lord Ashburton, is a very strange man."

"Ah, the Ra cult. I would believe anything about those warlocks. So, you all were engaged in some international intrigue or another. I see. And what was your destination?"

"Ultimately," Tom answered, "to get back to Bayern to make my report."

"I'm afraid you will be delayed," said Nemo. "This ship is engaged in a series of tests of new equipment which cannot be interrupted. Once the testing has run its course, I will be happy to put you ashore anywhere you please, though it will have to be along the coast, by dinghy. I do not care to be caught in the shallow waters of any harbor."

Tom shrugged. "I certainly can't expect the *Nautilus*, of all craft, to be a passenger ship."

"I am glad you understand," Nemo said. "Now, gentlemen, after that ducking in stormy waters, you might be wanting a drink." Nemo touched a button on the side bulkhead. In a few moments, an orderly came in and Nemo instructed him to serve the guests a drink from a built-in liquor cabinet.

"You'll forgive me if I don't join you," Nemo said. "I, myself, am a total abstainer, in addition to being a strict vegetarian."

"I once knew a vegetarian chap," Brewster piped up. "Wouldn't eat fish, either."

"I used to eat fish," Nemo said, "before realizing that fish is flesh, as well. Now, I consume only marine flora, including cultured algae. Speaking of which, you will, of course, be my guests at dinner."

"Oh, I say," Brewster said, taking a glass of wine. "Sounds absolutely toothsome. Can't wait to get my teeth into some algae. Hard to get good algae these days, you know." He drank.

Nemo smiled. "I do not insist that my guests, when I have them, share my peculiar eating habits. I believe the cook is serving sea bass in dill and lemon sauce tonight.

"What are these spirits?" van Helsing asked, peering into his glass. "It is most unusual."

"Distilled from a mash of kelp and other seaweeds," Nemo said.

"Topping stuff," Brewster said, through gritted teeth. "Smashing, absolutely smashing."

"It keeps the crew at bay," Nemo said. "Of course, I ration it judiciously."

"But, of course, you'd have to," Brewster said.

The dining room adjoined the salon. It, too, was elegantly appointed, for all its being aboard a spartan warship—and the *Nautilus* was a warship, one that made war on war itself.

Dinner conversation was desultory. Nemo's manner was subdued and somewhat distracted, as if a matter of great moment pressed on his mind. He ate his food without saying much of consequence, made his excuses, and said good night.

Tom regretted missing the opportunity of interviewing the strange man at length. He had many questions for Nemo about many things. Tom could see by the expression on van Helsing's face that he also felt that a rare chance had been missed.

Brewster ate his lemon bass and washed it down with iced desalinated sea water. He allowed as it was quite refreshing, if a little flat.

Back in their tiny cabin, the men discussed their options.

"Escape?" van Helsing said. "How?"

"Nemo's supposed to have underwater breathing gear," Tom said. "If we could get into the compartment where it's stored, we might literally be able to walk away from this ship."

"If we find the compartment, if we divine how to use the equipment, if we discover a way out of the ship . . ." Van Helsing threw up his hands. "It seems hopeless, Tom."

"Maybe so, but it's a possibility we can hold in reserve. Otherwise, we are stuck aboard this vessel until Nemo snaps out of the blue funk he's in."

"Blue funk? You mean his melancholia?"

"Yes. That's the word."

Van Helsing nodded. "From a medical standpoint, you are quite correct. It is the way of his ilk. Men of surpassing genius tend to be moody and unstable. I do not mean to imply that he suffers from dementia, but I would say that Nemo is a man who has deep-seated urges which no one can name, not even, perhaps, himself. I remember once discussing this with a fellow student of mine in medical school, in Vienna. He wanted to specialize in nervous diseases. He had some rather peculiar notions about—"

"I think he's balmy," Wynnie Brewster said. "Making his liquor from seaweed and eating pond scum. Then shutting himself into this steel leviathan without so much as a whiff of fresh air. A man oughtn't to do those things to himself. He's mad, I tell you."

"Judging by his behavior at supper," van Helsing said, "I would venture to diagnose him as having entered the acute phase of an obsessive hysteria. Of course, I can do no more than conjecture."

"We should find out what he's up to," Tom said. "I do have to get back to home base. Not that I have anything important to report." He stretched out in his bunk and laced his hands behind his head. "In fact, the only thing I have to report is total failure of my mission."

"Surely some good will come of your adventures thus far," van Helsing said reassuringly.

"Yeah," Tom said. "I'll know what not to do next time."

Thus began a dull routine aboard the *Nautilus*. The three castaways spent the morning in their cabin, then were conducted to the ship's general mess for lunch, after which they spent the afternoon in the salon, reading, staring out the observation window, playing chess on a magnetic board, and engaging each other in idle conversation. Before dinner they were permitted an hour in the gymnasium—it was small, little more than a compartment with a padded floor, some Indian clubs, and a chinning bar. Then, dinner in the mess.

These were mostly silent affairs. The crew was either not permitted to speak with the passengers, or they did not care to. Brewster, nevertheless, occasionally tried to chat up any crewman who was anything less than downright surly.

"I say, sailor. You there. What's the captain's game out in these waters? I mean, we seem to be after something. Is he chasing some Prussian dreadnought or another? Are we going to be ramming her?"

The sailor across the table did not look up from his bowl of fish stew.

Brewster tried again. "By the way, I've been meaning to ask, haven't gotten round to it, I haven't the foggiest notion what our position is, navigationally speaking, latitude and longitude, azimuth and right ascension, that sort of thing. Uh, sailor? Can you tell us where we are?"

"His game is Kraken," the sailor said, with a furtive glance over his shoulder.

"Well, he . . . what did you say, sailor? His game is what?"

"Kraken. The monster of the deep."

"Oh, kraken. Well, that explains it. Kraken, is it? Ripping good hunting, going out for Kraken. Gets the blood up, what?"

"A legendary sea monster," van Helsing said. "Out of Norse saga."

"Giant squid, maybe," Tom said.

"Wish it were," the sailor said. "Giant squid wouldn't faze me none. He's out for the real thing, the beast that lurks a thousand fathoms down. If I were you, I'd crawl in the life bell and cast off. He's . . . he's crazy, you know." This last in an awed whisper.

But he was nonetheless overheard. A crewman at the next table leaned over and said roughly, "Stow that mutinous talk, sailor."

The first man nodded, his face fearful. After wolfing down his stew, he got up and left without another word, nor a single glance at the passengers.

Back in the cabin, Tom was about to wash his face when he was startled by the sight of Marianne in the mirror above the washbasin. Not as startled as he'd been the first time, though.

"Tom, where on earth are you?"

"Not on the earth. Underwater, in Nemo's *Nautilus*."

"The *Nautilus*! How did you manage that?"

"Long story. No way to get off for now, I'm afraid. All I can report is that Lord Ashton Montague—"

"Morrolan says they may be listening."

"Then this little device is useless for reporting. Suffice it to say that it's been rough out here in the field."

"Tom, I'll keep calling periodically. Make sure you stay near a mirror. Any mirror."

"Will do. Over and out."

For two weeks, the *Nautilus* hunted its prey in the frigid waters of Scandinavia, and all the while the captain put his ship through constant diving runs. Each run took the submersible ship ever deeper.

"It is an obsession, surely," van Helsing diagnosed. "Under the guise of scientific curiosity is a compulsive urge to plumb the depths of existence, to reach down to its lowest, most primordial level. Perhaps it is the depths of the psyche, his own, that he wishes to sound. As I said before, this type of analysis reminds me very much of a chap I knew in Vienna. Jewish fellow, by the name of—"

"Mad, utterly stark, staring bonkers," Brewster mumbled. "Up and down, dive and surface, bells bonging all over the ship, shouting and tumult."

"Do you think there is a Kraken," Tom asked, "or is it a figment of his imagination?"

Van Helsing, standing at the observation bubble, turned to look out at the murky depths. "Who can say? Who can know what lurks at the bottom of the ocean? Or of the human soul. Nemo has dedicated his life to a cause. Now that he has temporarily suspended his relentless pursuit of absolute peace, something must arise to take its place. Hence, the search for the Kraken. As the Bible puts it, 'Deep calleth unto deep.'"

"If we only knew where the hell the life bell is," Tom said. "Has to be some means of escape."

"Failing that, old boy, I wish Nemo'd find the Kraken," Brewster said. " This routine is getting decidedly tedious."

"Maybe the Kraken will find us," van Helsing said.

CHAPTER 18

THE BEAST AT THE BOTTOM OF THE WORLD

The diving runs got quite deep. Nemo seemed bent on testing the ship to its limit. He would plunge the ship to the depths, then order the engines shut off. In the ensuing silence, the sounds of strain on the hull were all too audible. A horrendous creaking, a cry of distressed metal, filled the ship as the lowest point of the dive was reached. On each dive the sound grew more hideous, until it seemed that the hull would cave in and destroy everyone. These exercises strained the nerves of every man on board.

Then, after two and a half weeks of the quest and shortly after the day's diving had commenced, Nemo summoned the three castaways to the bridge.

"You have probably been wondering," Nemo said, looking through the eyepiece of some viewing device, "what we have been engaged in recently. As you see, the observation bubble on the bridge is shuttered. It can withstand the pressure of depths we have been attaining for only a limited time. So, I must peep out into the sea with a tube fitted with tiny lenses.

"You may well ask what I'm looking for. I will tell you. It is the greatest sea monster that lives. It is the beast. The leviathan. The very devil himself. It has lived in these waters since time immemorial. I want to see it; I want to verify its existence. For science, for the world. If there is any other task to which I have dedicated my life, besides the abolition of war, it is to discover the secrets of the natural world. This beast has haunted my dreams for years. Now, I am close to confronting it as a reality."

"Why?" Brewster asked. "I mean, every man needs a hobby, but why do it, Nemo, old boy?"

"It calls to me," Nemo said, now gazing inward.

"What will you do to the monster, Captain?" van Helsing asked.

"Do to it?" Nemo shrugged. "I will do nothing. I will observe it; I will take notes. What does any scientist do? I will take those notes and write a paper and have it published. But to do that I need data, facts based on reliable observation. I need witnesses as well. And if you will do me the honor of serving in that capacity, you will justify your presence aboard this ship."

"Well, Captain, we'd be delighted," Brewster said buoyantly. "Why if that's all you wanted, you should have said so in the first place. Pleased as punch to sidle up to this Kraken fellow of yours and give him a proper eye-clapping, for the record. Fascinating stuff, really. 'Deep calleth unto deep' and all that sort of thing."

"Thank you," Nemo said. "Unfortunately, the light at these depths is dim. We might have to open the shutters on the window momentarily."

"How do you know what's out there?" Tom asked Nemo.

"We track the beast by a revolutionary mechanism employing extremely high-pitched tones beyond the range of human hearing. The mechanism sounds these tones; they propagate through the medium of the water and reflect off any massive object. The time of the echo's return determines the distance of the object.

"Also, we have other listening devices operating. That is why we shut off the engine. You see this paper-covered drum? Notice the deflection of the needle. The beast is near. Very near." Nemo put his eye to the viewing device again.

"Fifty meters and closing," a crewman said.

"Continue all stop," Nemo said. "The beast knows we want it. It approaches to see who is curious about it."

"Thirty meters!" The crewman's voice rose in pitch.

"It comes," Nemo said, eye glued to the viewer.

"Ten meters!"

"I see it. But I must have witnesses. Open shutters on observation bubble!"

"Shutters opening!"

"Behold," Nemo said in an almost Biblical tone, pointing an almost accusatory finger at the hideous apparition appearing in the glare of the ship's external spotlights. "The Beast, the Enemy, the unspeakable excrescence that lurks at the heart of the world. Look on it, gentlemen, and be fearful."

What appeared was difficult for the eye to grasp and the mind to integrate. There was an eye, to be sure, an evil, monstrous thing like a gargantuan hard-boiled egg, ropy veins trailing from it. Surrounding this was a mass of writhing tentacles of a bewildering assortment of sizes: some as big around as tree trunks, some as thin as strands of pasta, all waving in the currents or wriggling with their own motion. This mass of quivering stuff began to envelope the *Nautilus*, and the eye pressed against the observation bubble.

"Good God," Wynnie Brewster said.

"Takes the breath away, does it not?" Nemo said, his tone now curiously detached.

"It does that," Wynnie agreed. "Uh . . . what now, Captain?"

"Full reverse!" Nemo shouted, and the first officer echoed him.

The ship's mighty engine whined as it backed the ship away. The monster receded quickly, waving its tentacles as if in farewell.

Everyone on the bridge breathed a little easier.

"Take her up to the surface," Nemo ordered. "We need fresh air and our electrical storage cells want recharging."

The *Nautilus* surged upward amid a flurry of bubbles.

"Thanks for the look at the Kraken," Tom said. "Do you think it poses a threat to shipping?"

Nemo said, "The legends say that it has done so in the past. Many a vessel down through the ages has disappeared with no apparent explanation. I am willing to speculate that the beast has taken its toll over the centuries."

"Centuries?"

Nemo nodded. "There is only one Kraken, Mr. Olam. It is an ancient, primordial form of life. The creature you saw is the same one that menaced sailors in mythological times."

"It should think about retiring," Brewster said.

"You should think about where you want to be put ashore," Nemo suggested.

"I suppose you can't be persuaded to enter the Central Sea," Tom said.

Nemo shook his head. "Under no circumstances. Much too shallow, I am afraid. The Prussians have been tracking our movements by airship. Our curiosity about their rocket firings have made them especially resentful of my presence. Any time we come to the surface, there seems to be a Prussian aerial man-o'-war hanging about. I will take the chance now because we are in deep water here, and we have just about exhausted our energy reserves."

The ship continued to rise.

"If you men desire a breath of fresh air, stay on the bridge. If not, you may go below now."

"I say, it'd be lovely to have a zephyr play about my nostrils for once," Brewster exclaimed. "Been cooped up for weeks. If you don't mind, Captain?"

"By all means. That is, if the area is clear."

"The Kraken was fairly deep, wasn't it?" Tom asked. "Can the Prussians detect us at that level?"

"Our bubble trail gives us away," Nemo said. "A trained observer with a field glass can track us in a calm sea. And when we discharge water from our ballast tanks, as we have just done, we create a storm of bubbles."

"Fifty meters!"

"Take us up to periscope depth," Nemo ordered.

The ship continued surging upward at a steep angle for another minute, then leveled off.

"Raise periscope," Nemo said.

A tube running from deck to overhead began to slide upward, but stopped.

"What is it?" Nemo said irritably.

"Periscope assembly is jammed, sir," a sailor reported.

"Very well," Nemo said. "We shall have to risk a blind surface. Open the observation bubble, and get lookouts up through the hatch as soon as we broach. Don't lose any time."

"Aye aye, sir!"

The ship rose again. The covering over the observation bubble retracted, and light spilled into the bridge.

The ship came to the surface, and Nemo stepped forward to get a look out the observation bubble. He did not need much of a look.

"Lookouts below! Dive, dive!"

The ship came alive with shouts, the clanging of hatches, the whirring of valves, and the hiss of air compressors. Sailors scrambled down the ladder from the hatch above.

"What is it, Captain?" Tom asked.

"Prussian dreadnought, waiting for us. Probably a whole flotilla nearby, ready to gang up on us. We'll have to run."

The ship plunged back into the sea. Water sluiced over the observation bubble as its shutters closed once again. The deck tilted steeply, and everybody on the bridge grabbed handholds to keep from pitching forward.

"Do not be alarmed, gentlemen. The *Nautilus* can outrun any ship in any navy in the world."

Suddenly, an explosion shook the ship. To Tom, it seemed like being inside a trash can and having someone whang it with a shovel. He pitched to the deck, and when he got up again, his ears were ringing like a telephone.

"Depth bombs!" Nemo said. For the first time, the castaways saw a flicker of emotion cross Nemo's countenance. It was not fear; it was concern, mixed with a genuine surprise. "They've finally tumbled onto the only way one fights a submersible ship. Timed depth charges."

Those pesky Prussians are really starting to annoy me, Tom thought.

Another underwater explosion sent everyone sprawling on the deck. A pipe sprang a leak, spewing water all over.

"Take her down!" Nemo shouted. "Maximum depth!"

The ship sank until the hull again began to complain, creaking its protest against the awful pressures of the deep.

More depth charges went off, but these were not as close. Seconds later, a salvo of them detonated, but ineffectually far above the ship.

Sailors succeeded in valving off the leak, and some sense of normality returned to the bridge.

"All ahead full. Continue dive to maximum depth," Nemo ordered.

"Aye, sir."

"I suggest you men go below," Nemo said to Tom. "We will simply slip out from under them and surface again. You'll be called when we do."

"Thanks, Captain. I hope the new depth bombs don't cramp your style. I mean, pose a permanent threat," said Tom.

"I have already thought of a few countermeasures," Nemo said, smiling. "But the main one is not to be caught in a trap again. I'm afraid my preoccupations with marine biology have distracted me overmuch. But that is easily—"

The ship seemed to run smack into something. Tom, Nemo, and everyone else were thrown toward the bow. Tom hit the forward bulkhead hard, injuring his knee. Nemo caught himself on a handhold and hit a control.

The observation bubble opened to reveal a huge inhuman eye, like a poached egg, peering in.

"The Kraken!"

"All reverse!" Nemo yelled.

The submersible's engines slammed into reverse. The *Nautilus* struggled to get free of the creature's clutches, furiously churning the water with her mighty screws. The creature pressed its attack, its multitudinous tendrils swarming over the ship, trapping it in a writhing web of death.

"Electrify the hull!" Nemo shouted.

Tongues of electricity licked out from the ship, and the creature spasmed.

"Again!"

Once more, miniature bolts of lightning played amongst the monster's forest of appendages. Beneath the eye, a hideous V-shaped mouth opened in a silent scream of pain.

The ship began to descend, but not of its own volition. The stunned creature was dragging it down.

A spray of water hissed through the edges of the observation window, wetting down the bridge.

· "Close shutters!"

The shutters, iris like, mercifully closed off the view of the Kraken, and the leaking stopped.

But other leaks sprang inside the bridge and on the lower decks. Shouts of the crew rose up, along with the sound of running feet. There came another sound, that of metal stressed beyond its limits, as the ship descended to pressures it was not designed to withstand.

"Blow all tanks! Surface! Forward screws, all ahead full!"

Nemo rocked the ship back and forth in a desperate effort to free her, but the dead weight of the creature continued to drag it down.

Nemo turned to Tom and his companions. "Get aft, use the life bell! Bay number thirty-seven, Deck B—save yourselves, if you can!"

They obeyed, clambering down the ladder to the lower deck.

"Wish he'd showed us what and where the life bell is," Tom said.

"But the pressure at this depth," van Helsing said. "We won't survive."

"We sure won't survive inside this deathtrap. Let's find thirty-seven B."

They made their way toward the rear of the ship, sloshing through oily, ankle-deep water and dodging vents of scalding steam. The crew did not seem to be in a panic. They hurried to their various emergency stations, some busily valving off fractured pipes.

"Here!" Tom shouted, finding the right door.

"You're jumping ship!"

Tom stopped. It was the crewman they'd talked to in the mess.

"Come with us," Tom said. "Save yourself."

The man made a motion to enter the compartment, but halted himself. "No," he said, shaking his head. Some internal conflict seemed about to tear him apart. His eyes were filled with fear, but something more powerful held him in check. "No! He . . . he would not want it. He would not . . . forgive."

"Suit yourself, my good man," Brewster said.

The three castaways piled into the compartment, and Tom closed the hatch and dogged it. The sound of clanging alarms receded.

"What's up there?" Brewster said, pointing.

"The bell," van Helsing said. "Up the ladder!"

The ladder led up through a tube into a small spherical compartment just big enough for three bodies. Tom was the last one up. Brewster and van Helsing pushed the central hatch down. As they did, they could see a lower hatch sliding closed to seal off the bay below. They sat on the upper hatch while Tom dogged it shut.

There was a red lever clearly marked Launch Bell. Tom gave it a pull, and the bell began to rise, detaching from the *Nautilus*.

After inspecting the interior, Tom said, "Near as I can figure, everything's automatic. The bell will rise to the surface by itself, very slowly, to adjust for pressure. Let's just hope the Kraken doesn't want *hors-d'oeuvres* before it eats the *Nautilus*."

"I can't even see the *Nautilus!*" Brewster yelled, looking out the bell's small view plate. "It's gone!"

Tom peered out. He could see nothing but clouds of bubbles, a few blobs of light, and the almost infinite mass of the Kraken.

The bell rose, agonizingly slowly. Presently, there was nothing outside the view plate but darkness.

Half an hour went by before the darkness outside ameliorated to dim murk.

"Any water aboard this tub?" Brewster asked. "I'm parched."

Tom opened a small compartment built into the bulkhead. Inside were small packages and a few metal flasks. He handed one of the flasks over to Brewster.

"Ah, desalinated salt solution. Yummy. Who was this dandy device intended for? Nemo, himself?"

Van Helsing shook his head. "For any innocents that happened to be aboard. Nemo is nothing if not a moralist. The bell was certainly not for the crew. They are tragically enmeshed in his obsession."

"Just what obsession is that, good Doctor?" Brewster asked.

"They are all in the grip of a death wish. Is that not obvious? Their profession is death. Nemo is obsessed with it. He craves it, yet he fights against it. The Kraken is merely the embodiment of this deep-seated desire to merge with the universe, to commune with, as the Greeks put it, *Thanatos.*"

"Oh, I say, that's miles above my head, old bean. Amazing, though, that sailor bloke, not getting in with us when he had the chance."

"The father figure must be obeyed. Conscience is sometimes stronger than the urge for survival," van Helsing said.

"Food in here, too," Tom said, handing packages around.

Brewster took one, opened it to find squares of an unidentified greenish substance. He ate one. "Ah, finally we get to sample the seaweed glop."

"The complete lifeboat," van Helsing said, looking about in admiration. "Ingenious. The man is a mechanical wizard. And this hatch, above, is the way out, I suppose."

"Right," Tom said. "But we have to surface first, which . . ." He glanced out the view plate. "Should be coming up, eventually. I can see blue up there, somewhere."

Finally, the life bell broached the surface and bobbed in the waves. The sea was calm, but the tiny bell-shaped escape craft was not exactly a pleasure yacht. The survivors got jostled a bit. Still, it was tolerable.

But it was just barely tolerable for three whole days, during which the little bell craft bobbed and drifted. Brewster was the sickest, constantly having to relieve himself from the top hatch. On the third day, he came down with dry heaves, having nothing left to heave up. Tom and van Helsing were seasick as well, but handled it much better. All three were black and blue from the constant motion of the waves. The life bell had not really been designed as a lifeboat. The food ran out toward evening of the third day, but no one had any appetite. Then, just as the sun was about to set:

"I see a ship," van Helsing said.

"Excellent," Brewster said. "Ouch." He had banged his temple against the bulkhead.

"Prussian," van Helsing said. "A dreadnought."

"Blast."

"Total failure," Tom said, shaking his head.

"Here, here, old boy, keep your pecker up. Don't fret." Brewster urged. "We're shipwreck survivors. They have an international obligation to treat us right, don't they?"

"In your case, yes. For me, it'll be different. Every Prussian secret service operative will be alerted that I'm to be held for interrogation. If there's one aboard this ship, I'm sunk."

"I hope not, " van Helsing said. "And, in spite of everything, I do hope Nemo is not sunk either."

CHAPTER 19

PROGRESS

"Two weeks!"

Tarlenheim stared in disbelief at the strange craft taking shape on the cavern floor below.

The exterior was complete. The shape of *Numero Due* was similar to its prototype's, but a bit fatter. It rested on two sledlike runners. The ends of rotating blast nozzles hung on the craft's underside. A panoramic view window extended across the broad nose.

It was a big ship, crowding out everything on the factory floor below. Above, an immense ventilation hatch, arranged in orange-slice sections, waited to open and release the craft into space.

"I don't believe it," Tarlenheim went on. "I knew dwarfs worked fast, but this—"

Zambelli and Marianne flanked him. They were almost as astonished at the project's progress as he was, though Morrolan had told them to prepare for a small miracle. He knew dwarfs quite well.

"A miracle," Zambelli said, dabbing his face with a handkerchief. The temperature inside the dwarfhold was frequently elevated. "Sorcery!"

"No, dwarf industry," Tarlenheim said.

"No, sorcery," came Morrolan's voice behind their backs. They turned.

Smiling furtively, Morrolan came to the rail and looked down. "They had a little help. From me."

"I knew it," Zambelli said. "The devil's work."

"Oh, no, just a hurry-up spell, the kind that any crone might cast to make the housework go faster."

Zambelli crossed himself.

"Remarkable, in any event," Tarlenheim said. "Rhyme tells me it is almost ready to fly."

"There will be a short testing period," Morrolan said, "combined with a rescue attempt. Rather dicey, but there you are."

"Tom is in trouble. I have not been able to contact him in a week."

"He is probably still a virtual prisoner aboard Nemo's undersea boat," Tarlenheim said.

"No. Something has happened. I can feel it. Morrolan, can you . . . I mean . . . is it possible—?"

"Spellnap him here? Of course. But it might take months to devise the thaumaturgics. Across great distances, teleportation spells are tricky. Very, very tricky. Nevertheless,

I am working on something. My dwarfs have installed the magic mirror aboard ship, along with an arrangement of light baffles."

"Light baffles?"

"Prisms arranged in a certain mathematical relationship. I know nothing of optics, however. One of the dwarfs helped immensely. Starlight Lensmaker is his name. The technical side of the device is purely his invention."

"It is a magnificent ship," Marianne said.

"I hope it works," Tarlenheim said. "*This* is our answer to the Prussian rocket threat."

"I have a feeling," Morrolan said, "that the threat is not as ominous as you suspect. All you need to do is confront the Prussians with this . . ."

"Of course!" Tarlenheim exclaimed. "They'll soil their breeches, they will."

Morrolan laughed. "With this you could shoot their firecrackers out of the sky. Well, not really, but they don't have to know that."

"I've been a dunce," Tarlenheim said. "This is a battle of bluff and bluster. I never thought the Kaiser would consent to bombarding women and children, for all that I think him as much a rotter as Bismarck. But he is not past allowing Bismarck to threaten us with extinction. Well, we can threaten right back. And we don't have to bombard women and children. We can drop a fifty-pounder right into old Ironbottom's privy, if we so desire."

"That's the spirit," Morrolan said, slapping the colonel's back.

"I still want to go to the moon," Zambelli said, a little wistfully.

CHAPTER 20

TOM IN BONDAGE

The next few days fell into a dreary routine as the castaways were shuffled from one organ of the Prussian state to the next, from one interrogation to the next. They were questioned first by the naval intelligence officer aboard the dreadnought.

"Thomas Bond" and his companions had concocted a story in the minutes before the life bell had been winched aboard the Prussian battleship. They had been out sailing in the English channel on Brewster's yacht when the surfacing *Nautilus* had inadvertently smashed it to pieces. The rest of the story hewed more or less to reality, except for mentioning the Kraken and Nemo's possible demise along with that of the *Nautilus* and its crew. They had made their escape in the life bell when a power failure plunged the ship into darkness.

Not that Tom Olam expected the Prussians to believe it. It merely gave Tom something to repeat endlessly to one interrogator after another: after navy intelligence came the Bremerhaven police; then a Prussian foreign service representative came to participate; after that, Prussian army intelligence men arrived to cart them away to an army base near Hamburg. Whereupon, one short interview later, they were put on a train, accompanied by plainclothes guards, and sent to Berlin. Tom sat out several opportunities for escape. All seemed doomed to eventual failure. The Prussians were not about to let him go.

Brewster never stopped demanding to see a representative of the British consulate and was, of course, consistently ignored.

"We were in international waters, blast it all," Brewster complained to the Foreign Service interrogator.

"Lies!" the interrogator shouted. He was a fat man with a florid face and a ridiculous haircut, the side of his head almost shaved clean and the top in short spikes. "You were picked up well within the territorial limit claimed by his Imperial Majesty the Kaiser. You are spies. You tried to enter this country surreptitiously in a submersible craft cleverly disguised as a channel marker buoy. This story about Nemo and the *Nautilus* is sheerest fantasy. I, myself, have never believed those stories by that ridiculous French scribbler. Nemo is a myth! You will now tell me the truth or you will face the direst consequences."

"I tell you, it's the truth, you bloody twit!"

Wynnie Brewster had not used profanity up to this point, Tom noted.

Then, suddenly and without another word, Berlin was done with them, and they were herded aboard a private railroad car and shipped east. The journey took an entire day. At the end of the line, they were turned over to more army personnel, rank and file soldiers this time, and taken by horse and wagon to an installation very near the Baltic coast. The military base was little more than a collection of featureless concrete buildings half sunk into the ground. On a hill overlooking all the concrete and grimness was an imposing neo-Gothic stone manor.

Tom knew where he was. He knew a secret rocket test facility when he saw one. The launching pads lined the beach. The manor doubtless had belonged to the late Wilhelm Friedrich von Bremen.

They were thrown into a cell deep underground. And there they stayed for several days, eating wretched food and sleeping in lumpy bunks, before they had a visitor.

"Herr Hauptmann. How nice to see you again."

"Much more pleasant circumstances than our last meeting, I must say," Hauptmann said in perfect, if clipped English. "At least, for me. Are you comfortable here?"

"As a bloody pasha, old bean," Brewster sneered. "This is a veritable seraglio, can't you see?"

"Mr. Brewster. I find it frankly absurd that you could be a spy, but Berlin seems to think otherwise. You will probably not be hanged. Although you are not titled, you are a scion of a noble British line, and between Germany and England there is an aristocratic bond, of sorts. You will most likely continue to enjoy the hospitality of His Imperial Majesty for some time to come."

"Well, thank my cousin the bloody Kaiser for me, will you?"

"I shall. Dr. van Helsing, I have never heard of you before, but there must be a reason for your part in all this. What information I have is not complimentary. You have been known to consort with certain intellectuals and bohemians of an unsavory and decadent stripe. You are very probably a threat to the realm, but I cannot put my finger on the nature of it. Fear not, I have ample time to think it through."

Hauptmann took a few steps toward the right side of the cell, his polished black boots clicking against stone. "Now you, Captain Olam, are a different case entirely."

"Natch."

"You are military personnel, in mufti, attempting to enter the country by stealth. You are a spy."

"A shipwreck survivor. Otherwise, you have nothing on me."

Hauptmann took a paper out of his jacket and opened it. "On the contrary, you are an internationally sought criminal on a crime spree, it seems. You are wanted by the French police for assault, attempted murder, and the theft of a private vehicle. Scotland Yard wishes to consult you on a matter of attempted burglary and the vandalizing of certain valuable art objects.

"You are charged with unlawful flight from the country, and, strange as it seems, they want you in connection with the mysterious disappearance of Mr. Brewster, here. Well, that is, of course, of no consequence, but we will not be telling them otherwise, for our own reasons. Last, but not least, you are guilty of attempted espionage. And that is entirely *leaving* aside the matter of your part in the dastardly attack on His Majesty's Airship *Gotland*."

"All trumped up," Tom said.

"Certainly. But do not think for a minute that we have nothing. We have a great deal. However, your ultimate fate really does not concern me. You are here in Peenemünde as my guest, to witness my triumph. It is the end of your quest, as well. You wanted to know about our rocket program, and you will find out. Everything. You will witness the final field test of our prototype rocket bomb, the Model A-60. Or as it has been redesignated, the Kaiser's Vengeance Two. The KV-2. Although His Majesty has declined the invitation, the Reich's Chancellor will be in attendance."

"You're taking a big risk, Rupert, old friend, putting on a dog and pony show."

"No risk, at all. The system has been perfected. We have not had a failure so far."

"It's all a bluff. You have no guidance system."

"We do. A simple but ingenious one. With it, the KV-2 can pinpoint any target, military or civilian, within five hundred kilometers. And when the KV-3, the two-step rocket, is built and perfected, no target within five thousand kilometers will be safe. In time, as the rocket program progresses, there will be no place on earth beyond our reach. And there is no defense against this weapon, Olam. No defense possible."

"Congratulations."

"Thank you. And now, I see it is just about dinnertime. Enjoy your cabbage, gentlemen."

"Don't forget to thank Villy for us," Brewster shouted after Hauptmann, as the Prussian marched out of the cell block.

Dinner did indeed arrive shortly. The turnkey opened the barred door and a corporal wheeled in dinner, three bowls of sauerkraut, three heels of bread, three cups of lukewarm coffee.

"Sauerkraut," Brewster said, his pug nose upturned. "I hated the stuff before I got sick of eating it."

"Any ideas, Thomas?" van Helsing asked, after the corporal and turnkey had departed.

"One. I can pick that lock easily. But from there it will be improvisation. I suggest we wait till nightfall."

"You have a pick?"

Tom held up a slender metal rod with an L-shaped end.

"Where have you been keeping it?"

"Trade secret," Tom said, then promptly hid the thing under the mattress of his cot. "Well, let's eat. Then, we sleep. And tonight . . ."

"We have heartburn," Brewster said, brooding over his sauerkraut.

CHAPTER 21

BEHIND THE VEIL

"Wynnie."

"Uh?"

"Wynnie?"

"Ummm."

"Wake up, old sport."

Brewster's eyes opened, and he saw Tom's face floating before him in the darkness. "Right-o."

Brewster swung his legs and got up from the bottom bunk. The cell door was wide open.

"You did that marvelously," Brewster said.

"Let's go. There's another door."

Van Helsing was working on the cell block door. As the two other men approached, van Helsing pushed it open gently and peeked out.

Tom patted his back.

"I had some acquaintances in the Viennese underworld," van Helsing whispered.

Tom put a finger to his lips. Van Helsing nodded. He gave the same sign to Brewster, who also nodded.

Tom was first out into the corridor. At the end of it was a desk. The turnkey sat with his head propped up with both arms. Walking on tiptoes, Tom approached cautiously. Then he saw that the turnkey was asleep. Tom came up behind and hand-chopped the base of his neck, provoking a strange delayed reaction. The man woke up with a start, turned his head slightly and began to rise, but then slumped over the desk.

Tom opened a desk drawer. He found more keys, which he took, and some personal effects.

"Wynnie, here's your silver cigarette case."

"Blasted thieves. Van Helsing, these are yours."

"My wallet. They took the money."

"Be quiet, you guys."

Tom did not find his passport. Lack of one would make travel all the more difficult, but at the moment he deemed it the least of his problems.

In another drawer, he found a revolver, fully loaded.

Ho, ho.

They made their way down a long concrete tunnel that turned to the right at its end. The passage was illuminated every so often with gaslights. Most of it was in darkness. Continuing on, the passage made a series of right-angle turns before intersecting with another corridor.

"How far underground do you figure we are?" Brewster whispered.

"I estimated the lift went down four levels," Tom said. "But we can't risk using the lift. We'll have to find stairs. This way."

He led them to the left. The corridor went through another intersection, but Tom kept straight, not out of any hunch, but in a simple hope that he was making the right choice. He lucked out. At the end of the long passage was a stairwell.

He eased the door open. The stairs began on this level. Not a sound came from above. He went through the door and held it open for his pals. Then he eased the door closed. He pushed Brewster's and the doctor's heads together and whispered into their ears.

"Why are there no guards?"

They both shrugged silently.

"Could be a trap," Tom warned. "Watch it."

He led the way up the stairs and found he was right; there were four levels to the place. At the landing was a door with a window that looked out onto a vast production floor. Huge ballistic rockets in all stages of assembly filled the great domed hangar beyond the door.

"This is crazy," Tom said. "No guards. Has to be a trap."

"Perhaps we should toddle back to the cell and beg for amnesty?"

"They could spring the trap anywhere," Tom said. "I say we take our chances outside. Come on."

"Surely there are guards posted outside," van Helsing said.

"You'd think. Come on."

They went out to the vast production floor. These were well-constructed rockets. They resembled the WWII-vintage German V-2 of Tom's home universe, but with Victorian touches: they looked to be constructed mainly of tin sheeting with brass rivets; the nose cones were brass as well. Nevertheless, these weapons were essentially the V-2 seventy years before its "proper" time. And when the Unseelie manipulated things so that the Prussians would stumble onto liquid-fuel technology—and in only a few years, the Russian Tsiolkovsky would be inventing it in any event—they would be V-2s for all practical purposes.

And so on. And so on. Tom wondered if the Unseelie were even now agitating, in the physics laboratories of Prussian universities (or anywhere in New Europa, for that matter; physics was international), for nuclear fission.

V-2 plus a split atom equals . . . what? Armageddon? Or simply the Cold War eighty years before its time?

What were the Unseelie ultimately up to? An earth without human civilization, it seemed. Or perhaps a degenerate humankind that could be preyed upon like herds of wildebeest. Whatever they were up to, it was no good for the human race.

The three men came to the immense hangar doors, out of which would go the finished rockets.

There was a smaller door to the side. It had nothing but a simple deadbolt, which could be thrown from the inside.

"Makes no sense," Tom said aloud. "There's only one explanation."

"What's that, old son?"

"The security here is handled supernaturally. Phookas, sprites, sidhe, any spook that's hard to see. They patrol the place, see everything, and report."

"Which means . . . ," van Helsing said.

"Yes, that they're watching us, and it's definitely a trap. I want you two to go back to the cell. It'll probably make them wonder what the hell you're doing, and by the time they decide to do anything about it, you'll be back, and probably safe for the moment. I'm going out there to see this through to the end. It's me they want. Understand? The Unseelie have had a contract out on me ever since I arrived in this universe."

"Contract?"

"They want my blood. Or something. They don't wish me well, at any rate. I'm heading out. See you later, and good luck."

"See here, Olam," van Helsing said. "Our lives back in that cell couldn't be worth a farthing. I, too, want to see how this game plays out. I'm coming along, if you don't mind awfully much."

"That goes for me, Tommy," Brewster said. "Put me under starter's orders. I can keep a stiff upper, if you're worried about it."

"I know you can, old boy." Tom patted their shoulders, grinning. "There's two stout fellows. Let's go."

Tom undid the deadbolt and went out the door. Not even a cricket made a sound outside. A night breeze was blowing across the compound, coming in from the sea with a salty tang. Tom led the way across great expanses of tarmac, knowing that no guards were watching from watchtowers.

Or if they were, they were not hitting alarm buttons. No searchlights split the darkness, no shouts went up. It was as if he and his pals were walking across a vast movie studio lot, the huge concrete hangars standing in for soundstages.

They reached the edge of the compound and entered thick scrub brush that cleared out now and then for a sand pit or a grassy fairway. They were on links, the kind of land on which the game of golf had naturally developed. But Tom wasn't thinking of golf. He was thinking about what magical abilities he could bring to bear on the current crisis.

Answer. Doodly squaterino, as Zambelli might put it. Less than doodly squat. If only there was a way to send for supernatural help.

"I say, Tommy, old boy?"

Tom stopped. "Yeah?"

"I say, you might think me daft . . . well, I don't quite know how to say this . . . but—"

"Wynnie, spit it out."

"I keep hearing someone call your name."

"What?"

"Sounds as though I'm going round the bend, I know, but I'm dashed if I don't hear someone calling you."

Tom listened. Far away, surf broke upon the beach. Then, faintly, he heard it. He heard his name being called. But it wasn't . . . it wasn't far off in the night somewhere. It was somewhere very near.

He heard it again. It was . . .

Marianne! Now what in the blue-eyed world?

Suddenly the penny dropped.

"Wynnie, hand over your cigarette case!"

"My . . . are you sure?"

"Hand it over!"

Wynnie took the thing out and gave it up. And there, in the polished silver was Marianne's tiny image, as if on a television micro-receiver.

"Tom!" she exclaimed.

"Marianne!"

"Tom, we've been trying to reach you! Where on earth are you now?"

"Prussia, at Hauptmann's secret rocket installation. It's right on the beach. You can't miss it. Where are you?"

"Nowhere near. But we think we have a way to get you back. We're not quite ready yet, though. Oh, Tom, I've been so worried."

"Can you contact Auberon?"

"Morrolan might be able to." She paused. "Are you in trouble?"

"Lots. Tell him where I am and that the Unseelie are about to get me."

"I will."

"Got to go. I'm trying to escape."

"Whatever you do," Marianne warned, "keep that mirror or whatever it is you have."

"Check. Over and out."

A banshee wail went up to the rear. It made Tom jump.

"Let's run for it!"

The three men sprang into action, running over sand and sward, crashing through hedgerows of beach grass. But as they did, things gradually began to change in a remarkable way. The landscape transformed itself with unnatural speed.

The sky changed. Dead black gave way to dark turbulence shot through with blue light. The links faded, replaced by swirling mists, suffused with the same unworldly blue glow.

"Damn!" Tom stopped suddenly, and his pals slammed into him.

"I say, old man, this is getting more balmy by the minute."

"The Faerie Veil!"

Brewster stared at Tom. "What?"

"We must have run through a doorway, a Faerie doorway. We're not in the world anymore. We're in the Faerie Veil, the nowhere between universes."

"Remarkable," van Helsing said. "Utterly remarkable. A timeless place of nonexistence, the uncreated primeval chaos between the very sheaves of existence itself."

"Exactly," Tom said. "Where the Faerie originated, Seelie and Unseelie alike."

"Gadzooks, they live in this mess?"

"It is a mess, as you put it, only because we as humans lack the power to shape it to our needs," van Helsing said. "The Faerie can fashion of it whatever they desire."

"I'd go stark staring bonkers."

"Looks like somebody's fighting for control in this area," Tom said.

Two separate worlds appeared ahead, divided by an indeterminate, blurred line, like ill-matched mattes in a badly made motion picture. On the left stood drear, enchanted woods out of some Expressionist version of the Brothers Grimm. Dark and deep, but not very lovely. Boles of trees formed grotesque faces, trunks sprouted branches like flailing, grasping arms, and motile shadows busied themselves amongst prickly undergrowth.

To the right lay the bright fluttering fabric of eternal springtime, a world of sunny meadows, dappled glades, fields of flowers, and hills topped by quaint Faerie castles.

Tom tried to direct his feet rightward, but something curious happened. The more he ran for the good Faerie place, the more the good Faerie place receded behind the bad Faerie place. He broke into a desperate sprint, van Helsing and Brewster beside him, but it was no use. The tactic merely ensured their arrival in the dark woods, their shoes snapping dry, dead undergrowth until they came to a path of sorts. Having no choice, they followed its twisting way, smells of fungus and dry rot assailing their noses.

As the three men ran, the unearthly noises sounded all around them, increasing in intensity and number. Voices of unnamed things howled and screeched. Unnameable things answered, swelling the unholy chorus to an ear-splitting crescendo.

Tom could still see light coming through the trees. He veered right, off the path, crashed through a prickly bramble and instantly regretted his rashness. He was caught. He thrashed and kicked, but the barbs dug deeper into his flesh.

"Tommy, help!" came Wynnie's cry behind him.

"Hold on!" Tom yelled, wondering what he was supposed to do. Well, he was supposed to get himself free and help Wynnie, wasn't he? So he grabbed hold of something, a clutch of thorns, clinging vines, and stinging tendrils, and ripped with all his might. An agonized scream pierced the night, but he kept pulling on something alive, something that tugged back. He dug in his feet and yanked until something snapped and sent him tumbling backward, out onto the path. Getting up, he saw Wynnie's problem and dashed for him.

Trees, living trees, had Brewster wrapped up in gnarled branches like great, spidery hands.

"Let me go! I say, leave off me, you bloody bunch of toothpicks!"

Tom picked up a piece of dead wood and whacked at the things, and they shrank back, snarling. He kept whacking until they let Wynnie go.

"Where's van Helsing?"

"Here!" came the doctor's voice.

A species of snakelike vine had the Dutchman by the feet. Tom applied his cudgel to them and they writhed and twitched, then finally retracted.

Van Helsing got up on unsteady legs. "I haven't much stamina."

"Light, over there. Try to get to it."

"Or die trying," Wynnie said.

They tried, but Wynnie got entangled again almost immediately and had to be pulled out of clinging grass. Van Helsing got himself into a bog, and was sinking out of sight when Tom, trying to reach him, got snagged by brambles again. He couldn't move this time, much as he thrashed and writhed.

The thing that had him was at the base of something immense. Its shape was humanlike, but by its huge wings and preternaturally glowing eyes, Tom knew it for what it was.

The Unseelie Adversary, or some transmogrification of the same. Towering above Tom, it spoke in a voice like the crack of thunder.

"You annoy me, human. You will cease to annoy me very soon. I will see your carcass torn apart by fanged things you cannot dream about."

"Go back to the hell you came from!" Tom snarled. He struggled to reach the revolver tucked into the side pocket of his overalls. He did, finally, and pulled it out. He aimed at the Adversary and fired.

The monster howled.

Tom was puzzled, but he fired again. Again the Adversary seemed affected. The figure stumbled back and disappeared into the swirling mists. Tom fired again and again, until the revolver was empty.

He clicked the gun a few times, then threw it. He couldn't figure why the demonic creature would blink at a gunshot—unless. Unless the bullets contained some Cold Iron—meteoritic iron, which the Faerie feared, because it and it alone could deliver the True Death to immortals.

A small portion of the world's iron is meteoritic. Very small. Vanishingly small. Nevertheless—

Quite suddenly and inexplicably, the forest seemed to recede, as if it were a rug being rolled up and pushed aside. Tom found himself free, and van Helsing stepped up out of the bog.

Wynnie came out of the living grass picking stuff off his shirt. "What in blazes now, Tom?"

"We're getting some help," Tom told him. "It sure wasn't the gunshots."

"About blinking time. What's that?" Wynnie pointed ahead.

It was yet another world. It began abruptly where the enchanted forest stopped: a broad tilt of windswept, wildflowered meadow, bright and inviting.

"This looks okay," Tom said, stepping forward.

"Tom, don't do it!"

The voice had come from far behind. Halting, Tom spun and saw no one. But the voice was familiar.

"Don't go through to that world, Tom. It's a trick. Follow my voice."

It was Auberon.

"Auberon! I hear you!"

"Come here. I'll show you the right doorway."

"Follow me, men."

"Dogging your every step, old chum," Brewster assured him.

The three made their way through blue mist, following Auberon's voice. Presently, Auberon, flowing robes and all, coalesced out of chaos.

"This way," he said, turning. "Follow me."

"What's the game, Auberon?" Tom asked.

"They don't want the trouble with me that killing you would entail, so they've tried to shove you out of the Veil into some godsforsaken universe where you'd probably perish in a day or two—but that's not the same as their outright murdering you."

"I don't understand how we got into the Veil."

"Very nicely done, that," Auberon said. "You were sucked right into it. But I'll get you out."

"I say, he seems a splendid chap," Wynnie said, a little breathless for trying to keep up with Auberon's purposeful stride through the coiling blue fogs. Besides the figures of the three men and Auberon, there was nothing in this noplace but the fogs. Swirling fogs below and cyclonic fogs skyward, but nothing between, nothing but a vast emptiness, an inchoate absence of existence.

Something finally took shape ahead: a patch of sky, a night wind, a swath of sandy grass. The familiar world gradually returned, and Tom and his companions walked back into it.

Auberon, however, faded. Tom caught a glimpse of him standing off to one side, ushering his charges through a shimmering doorway that was more felt than seen. Tom did not stop to wave good-bye.

He stepped through and was back in Prussia, back on beach land, and it was still salt-tinged night along the coast of the Baltic Sea.

"Halt!"

Wynnie stumbled and fell. By the time he picked himself up, Prussian soldiers had him collared, as they had Tom and van Helsing.

Rupert Hauptmann stepped out from behind a clump of tall beach grass.

"Ah, there you are. You disappeared for a moment, but now we have you. Frankly, I am surprised to see you. I did not think you would be returning. I was more than ready to applaud your successful escape."

"I didn't fall for the trap, Hauptmann."

"You are infinitely lucky, Olam. However, that only means that you will not miss my little 'dog and pony show,' as you so colorfully put it. Tomorrow will be a special day."

"I say, Tommy, old boy," Brewster commented, "correct me if I'm wrong, but your chum Auberon seems to have crossed us up good and proper."

"Yes," Tom had to admit, genuinely bewildered. "He seems to have done just that."

CHAPTER 22

ROCKETS OVER PRUSSIA

"Ten . . . nine . . . eight . . . seven . . . six—"

"Why you count backwards?"

"—five . . . ah . . . what did you say?"

"How come you count backwards?"

Tarlenheim was seated in the commander's chair, directly behind the pilot's seat. To his left was Marianne, to his right, Morrolan, both seated; all three were strapped in. Rhyme was down below in the engine room. The pilot was Zambelli, who had stayed up two nights in a row studying the rocket's controls. Everyone agreed he was the only one for the job.

Tarlenheim twitched in his seat. "Why, I don't know exactly. It seemed the thing to do. I was merely preparing you to receive a command."

"What command?"

"I am the commander of this vessel. At least, I believe that was our agreement. I was giving you the command to set off."

"*Ma che cazzo.* Just say, 'Start the rocket.' Anyway, it's 'blast off.'"

Tarlenheim was visibly ruffled. He resettled himself in his chair, cleared his throat, and said, "Very well. Start the rocket and blast off. Please."

"*Si, presto, Comandante!*" Zambelli said crisply. Then, under his breath, "*Allemani tutti pazzi.*"

Tarlenheim leaned to Marianne. "What did he say?"

"He said Germans are crazy."

"I rather think the same of Italians."

"Humans are crazy," Steamfitter said to the dwarf standing at the rail next to him.

On the factory floor below, the rocket ship, now named the *Swanship Lohengrin*, shuddered and spat flames out of the nozzles running along its underside and rose off its sled-like runners. It made an awful din.

Steamfitter and the rest of the dwarfs who had been looking on ran for cover as the cavernous interior filled with smoke and fumes.

The rocket rose on pillars of fire, floating upward toward the open roof, the false peak of the mountain. It ascended through the opening and hovered in the sky for a moment. After wobbling a little, it shot forward, quickly disappearing from view.

The smoke billowed and flowed for half a minute, then began to dissipate. When it had cleared a bit and the sound of the rocket had faded, the dwarfs crawled out from underneath barrels and empty crates, then filed back through doorways into which they had ducked.

Steamfitter got to his feet, waving the fumes away. "Bah! It'll take a week to get the smell out."

The other dwarf sniffed and shrugged. "It doesn't smell so bad. Sort of like paraffin burning."

"I meant the humans. Leave the roof open for the rest of the day."

Rhyme's voice came through the sound-conducting pipe from the engine room. "The levitation spell is working to stabilize the ship."

"But she no feel so stable," Zambelli complained.

"You wouldn't be able to control the ship without the levitation spell," Rhyme said. "Believe me. The rockets are keeping us up in the air and moving us forward, but the levitation spell keeps us from flipping over and crashing."

"How's the engine she burn?"

"Burning is even and rate of fuel consumption is steady. The burning part of the spell is working fine."

"I do hope they know what they're doing," Tarlenheim said worriedly.

"Rhyme's outdone himself," Morrolan said.

"I wish I could understand it all," Tarlenheim said. "Explain it to me again?"

"Rhyme has one magical engine alternating three spells: levitation, burning, and invisibility."

"Tell me how that works again, please."

"It cycles through the three spells in the blink of an eye, many times a second. The result is three separate spells."

"But how can it—?" The colonel heaved a sigh. "All too complicated for me. Makes me nervous."

"It's the mechanical part that makes me nervous," Morrolan said. "That's what I'm worried about."

"Me, too, so I'm twice as worried as you."

"Well, we are flying. Aren't we?"

Tarlenheim craned his neck to look through the panoramic window. "We'll have to put in more windows. Yes, we are up in the air. Looks like the Starnbergersee, down there. We're traveling at a fairly good clip. Pilot, what's our speed?"

"I dunno. Fast!"

"You don't know how fast?"

"I'm too busy to look!"

"Very well. Report when you can."

"*Si, Comandante! Fammi una sega.*"

"I do wish he'd stop jabbering like that," Tarlenheim complained into Marianne's ear. "What did he say then?"

"He said something vulgar."

"Oh, he did, did he?"

The rocket ship flew, streaking through the skies of Bayern. Below, peasants and burghers alike looked up in alarm, searching the skies for the source of a horrendous, echoing roar like a mighty airborne church organ. Religious people, thinking the Last Trump was sounding, fell to their knees and prayed. No one saw a thing. Minutes later, a long trail of smoke gradually formed, like a gray twisting thread across the sky, but the delay was such that no one made any connection between sound and smoke.

The rocket was invisible.

The rocket crossed the entire breadth of the country in minutes, whooshing directly over Munich, and giving Landshut, Regensburg, and Nuremburg a close brush. The rocket buzzed Bayreuth as it skirted the southern tip of the Inner Sea, then hurtled into Prussia.

Zambelli finally glanced at the air speed indicator.

"*Madonna!*" He reached for the throttle and pulled it back. The screaming whine of the engine decreased in pitch to a steady hum.

"Yes, I was going to suggest," Tarlenheim said, "that we reduce speed before the ship breaks apart."

Zambelli nodded. "*Grazie, Signore.*"

"I hate to ask, but how fast were we going?"

"You don't wanna know!"

Tarlenheim sighed. "I knew I'd regret asking."

"I know I should have asked this before," Morrolan said, "but does anyone know exactly where we're going?"

"If the coordinates we have for the village of Peenemünde are anywhere near accurate," Tarlenheim said, "we'll get there. It's Zambelli's job to get us there. He has a compass in his instrument panel, and we went over the route endlessly. Where were you, Morrolan?"

"Helping Rhyme fiddle with his magical monstrosity."

"I hope the monster does not turn on us."

Marianne said, "I wish the maps we had were a little less ancient."

"A rocket test site should not be too difficult to find," Tarlenheim said. "Pilot, report our position!"

"We are flying," Zambelli said.

"Yes, I know. Where?"

"Over Prussia."

"I know that. Exactly where over Prussia?"

"We go too fast to say. Soon as I say we somewhere, we not there any more."

"*Ach!*" Tarlenheim said in despair.

"Don't worry. I find those rockets. I smell them."

"Give me strength, Lord," Tarlenheim prayed.

Without warning, the engine's hum began to fall off into a piteous dying wail. Zambelli threw some switches and yanked a toggle or two, but it made no difference. The engine was obviously shutting down.

"Rhyme!" Zambelli shouted into the voice tube. "Whatsa matter?"

"Something's wrong with the engine."

"*Come stupido!* What the hell is wrong?"

"I don't know. Might be a clog in the fuel line."

"*Che stronzo!*"

"Oh, dear," Morrolan said.

The bottom seemed to drop out from under everything. The ship lost its lift, and began to sink, but it did not dive toward the ground. It floated.

"We go down," Zambelli said almost apologetically. "We have to land."

"The invisibility spell will hold," Morrolan said, "but if we stay in one place too long, it might fade a bit."

"Thank heaven for the levitation," Tarlenheim said.

After about a minute of slow, wobbly descent, the ship nosed up sharply.

Zambelli yelled, "Hold on, we gonna hit a little hard!"

The ship slammed into the earth, bounced once, hit again, and slid a long, bumpy way to a stop.

"Ye gods," Morrolan complained when all was still.

Tarlenheim ordered the crew to report injuries. No one had any to report.

The colonel unstrapped and rose. "Morrolan, go aft and see if you can be of assistance. Marianne, we will exit the ship and stand guard."

"Yes, sir."

Tarlenheim went to the main hatch, unlatched it, and pulled it open. Outside was a pleasant hayfield, tall with winter-browned grass, spring-green shoots growing up underneath.

"Unstrap holsters," Tarlenheim ordered.

Marianne had her pistol drawn. "I don't have a strap on my holster."

"Marianne, not too trigger-happy, please. We don't want an incident unless we absolutely can't avoid it. Holster that firearm."

"Oh, all right," Marianne said a little petulantly, obeying.

After kicking down a rack of folding steps, Tarlenheim led the way down them and outside.

"*Ach!* Bayernese!"

Four men, farmers by the looks of them, stood near the nose of the ship, staring at the royal seal painted on the hull. On seeing Tarlenheim and Marianne come out, they backed away nervously. Two of them broke and ran to the right, disappearing from view behind the ship.

Marianne looked the ship over. "What happened to the invisibility?"

"Don't know. I'm inclined to believe it wasn't working in the first place. No matter, these clods don't look as though they'll be any trouble."

"But the other two are off to get the *gendarmes*," Marianne said.

"See here, what do you mean by landing this contraption in my field?" one of the farmers demanded after advancing boldly toward the intruders. He was a rotund man with a florid face and pale hair and eyes.

"Purely an accident, *mein Herr*," Tarlenheim answered pleasantly, pouring it on a trifle thick. "Sorry for the inconvenience. After we make repairs, we shall be on our way."

"But that doesn't give you the right . . . wait just a minute. You're an army man."

"Retired. As I said, our craft was on a test flight and we experienced a mechanical breakdown."

"It's invasion, that's what it is. You can't fool me. There's a regiment of cavalry bivouacked next farm over. I'll tell 'em about you, I will!"

Marianne whipped out her pistol. "If you're going to do things like that, farmer, you shouldn't announce it. Stay where you are or I'll shoot."

The man halted his backstepping. "But . . . you're a woman!"

"That will not prevent me from drilling a hole in you."

"I don't believe it."

The other man, much younger and thinner, said, "Go on, Uncle Franz, she won't. She's just a lady."

Franz was not persuaded. "Then . . . you go and get the cavalry, Willy."

"Uh, well . . ." Willy didn't budge.

Drawing his pistol, Tarlenheim said, "If she doesn't shoot you, I will. I'm afraid we'll have to detain you gentlemen for a moment. Please stay where you are."

"My sons will tell the police. You can't catch them."

"Well, let's hope we can effect repairs by the time the police arrive." Tarlenheim hadn't stopped smiling. "For your sake," he added, smile fading ominously.

"You won't get away with this," Franz warned indignantly.

"Marianne, while I'm entertaining our friends, see what the trouble is. Report back."

"Yes, sir."

Marianne hopped back up the steps, turned right and walked through a large compartment containing some curious apparatus arranged around an elevated platform like a stage. The far end of the compartment terminated in a hatch giving onto the engine room. Morrolan was on all fours just inside the hatch, peering into the baffling complexities of Rhyme's sorcerous engine.

"What's going on?" Marianne asked.

Morrolan shook his head. "Purely a mechanical problem, nothing I can do."

The rest of the engine room was choked with pipes and wires and arcane machinery that Marianne couldn't begin to understand. All she knew was that it was as hot as the devil and stank of burning stuff.

"What's wrong?" she asked.

Rhyme and Zambelli could hardly be seen, lost in a mechanical thicket of pipes, wires, coils, and spherical tanks. Zambelli was busy with a wrench, Rhyme with a screwdriver.

"Damned fuel line," Rhyme answered sourly.

"What happened to the invisibility?"

"Damned magic engine broke when we hit."

"Oh. Any chance of fixing it?"

"Damned if I know."

"We really must be airborne again very soon," Marianne warned. "The army's coming."

"We work as fast as we can," Zambelli said through clenched teeth.

"Can you fix it?"

"I can fix, I can fix!" Zambelli yelled. Then he skinned a knuckle, dropped his wrench, and let loose a torrent of Italian blasphemy.

"Careful about that stuff around sorcerous engines," Morrolan warned. Remember what Dante said about the damned in Hell: *"Bestemmiavano Dio e lor parenti, / l'umana spezi e 'l tempo e 'l seme / di lor semanza e di lor nascimenti."*

"And you know what I say to Dante?"

"What's that?"

"Vafungul!"

"Be careful," Marianne said, shrugging and wishing she could do something to help.

Zambelli took his sore finger out of his mouth. *"Grazie, Contessa!"* The irony nearly dripped.

Marianne went back to the main hatch and poked her head out before descending the steps. She did so just in time to see one of the young men who had run off now charging from behind at an unsuspecting Tarlenheim.

"Colonel!"

Marianne drew her gun and leaped down from the hatchway, but before she had taken two steps, she heard the scuff of a shoe against metal above and behind her. Before she could turn, the other boy came jumping down on her, hitting her full force. Her pistol went flying, and suddenly she was prostrate on the ground, gasping for breath, a great weight pinning her.

"I got her, I got her!"

Marianne wrenched her head around to get her face out of the dirt, spat out hay, and tried to twist her body, but the boy on top of her was enormously heavy, and she could not get leverage to flip him off. His breath came sourly into her ear.

"So, *Liebchen*, you like to fight, eh? What's a nice girl like you doing in pants, eh? And such nice pants, nice and filled out."

"Get off me, you big . . ." Her right arm was free, but mostly useless. Both shoulders were pinned fast.

The boy, about eighteen and with more muscle than fat, but lots of fat, laughed lewdly, and pressed the middle of his body into Marianne's posterior, lasciviously rubbing himself against her.

"*Espèce de salaud!*"

"Oh, calling us pet names in French, are we?"

"*Allez, foutre le camps!*"

"Ohhhhhh, I like it, I like it. Tell me more."

Marianne finally succeeded in wriggling her hand to where it needed to be, right below the small of her back. She grabbed the boy's testicles and squeezed as hard as she could.

The boy yelled and rolled off her. Marianne flipped and brought her left fist down hard on the boy's nose.

The next half minute was devoted to a short but furious dust up; the colonel and Marianne versus three heavy set bumpkins bent on defending the Fatherland from foreign invasion. Bumpkins they were, but they fought arduously, if a little oafishly. Willy and the other boy were wiry and almost as strong as the sex maniac. Willy and Franz ganged up on Marianne. After Willy was disabled by Marianne's high kick to the teeth, the fight became a little fairer. Franz was big, but slow.

Tarlenheim boxed with Franz's other son and acquitted himself admirably for a man of his age. He blocked a few haymakers, then delivered a right cross that laid the boy out cold.

Marianne preferred to kick-box, in the Gallic fashion. She was about to take Franz out with a whirling kick, but out of the corner of her eye caught sight of the beefy sex maniac scrabbling in the hay for something, blood still bubbling from his nose.

She took three balletic leaps toward him and arrived in time to kick her pistol from his hand and follow up with a hand chop to the back of his neck. Deferring a reach for the gun, she whirled to deliver the kick reserved for Franz, who obliged graciously by running his protruding beer-belly into her foot. He whoofed, eyeballs rolling up white, and dropped.

The fight was over. Tarlenheim searched around for his gun, stooped, and fetched it out of the hay. Marianne retrieved her firearm.

"This is turning into a fiasco," Tarlenheim complained. "Are we ready to blast off again?"

"Zambelli says he can fix it."

"Can he?"

"I haven't the slightest."

"I should have known better than to trust some crazy Italian inventor," Tarlenheim muttered. "This will never do."

"At least Franz and the boys won't be running to tell anyone."

Just as Marianne said it, a Prussian zeppelin came soaring over the treetops. It made a peculiar sound for an airship. And the reason was that it had no propellers. Instead, it vented high-pressure steam out a single pipe protruding from its tail. The craft was, after a fashion, rocket-propelled. Its Gatling guns immediately began to chatter.

"*Gott in Himmel!*" Tarlenheim yelled, stamping his boot. He was decidedly bothered. "Yet another infernal machine. Into the ship!"

As bullets thumped into the dirt and pinged off the hull, Tarlenheim complained bitterly, "I don't believe I went up in this pile of scrap. There's not a gun aboard her! Most unmilitary!"

"We didn't have time," Marianne offered lamely.

Tarlenheim entered the hatch and was promptly knocked down by Zambelli, who was rushing forward. "Damn it all to hell!" Tarlenheim thundered.

"*'Scusi, 'scusi!* Everyone strap in, I'm-a gonna blast!"

"Do so immediately!" Tarlenheim shouted at the top of his lungs.

The Italian wasted no time. No sooner did Morrolan, Tarlenheim, and Marianne buckle their straps than a tremendous acceleration slammed them back into their seats. The rocket whooshed over the hayfield and fairly jumped at the sky.

The steam-rocket zeppelin flew directly into its path.

"Look out, you idiot!" Tarlenheim screamed.

Zambelli rammed the rocket ship through the zeppelin's air sac, cutting through it like a Saracen sword through a Damascus carpet. There came a vast tearing and a great fluttering of fabric against the forward windows. A ball of flame whooshed into existence, then dispersed.

The rocket, entirely unscathed, blasted due east into Prussia, leaving the flaming wreckage of the zeppelin behind to drop at its leisure.

CHAPTER 23

THE OTHER ROCKET

By morning, Tom had it finally figured out—almost. Auberon had been responsible for spellnapping Tom out of his home universe, the world where Faerie was fantasy, not reality. Auberon's plan, as far as Tom had been able to puzzle it out, had been to provide this universe, where Seelie and Unseelie vied for control but were locked in a sort of Mexican standoff, with input from other universes, something quite unprecedented in Faerie history. The various universes of historical happenstance were usually closed to one another, incommunicado, few having any clue even that other alternatives existed.

The complete reasoning behind Auberon's plan still eluded Tom, but it surely had something to do with the notion of transplanting a man from the future into the still growing garden of New Europa. Give him a little help, and he could provide the human husbandry necessary to nip in the bud the horrors that had grown wild in other, similar, soils.

Something like that.

So, Auberon had saved Tom from stepping off the Faerie Veil into oblivion and probably death. And he had shooed him along the proper path back to Falkenstein and New Europa. But why didn't he drop Tom off back in Bayern while he was at it? He surely could have managed that trick.

That part of it, Tom did not understand at all.

"Good morning, gentlemen!"

Hauptmann was all cheer and smiles and full dress military splendor, spiked Prussian helmet and all. "Had your breakfast, I trust?"

Wynnie Brewster let out a tremendous belch. "Pardon me," he said.

Hauptmann admonished him with a disapproving frown. "Really, Brewster, I thought that sort of juvenilia past you."

"There's not a lad come out of English public school who can't burp on cue."

"An outstanding achievement. If I may continue—"

"Please do, Fritz, old chap."

"*Colonel Hauptmann*, if you please."

"Sorry. Do blather on."

"This is a festive occasion," Hauptmann said.

Wynnie farted, quite loudly.

Hauptmann took a dim view of this. "I am determined," he continued quietly, "that you will join me in celebrating three years of hard work, perseverance, and struggle. Today marks a new era in Prussian military history. Indeed, in world military history. The Age of the Rocket is at hand, and I personally have ushered it in. The triumph is mine. So will be the glory. And to mark that occasion, I have provided, first, some refreshment . . ." He clapped his hands, and two soldiers wheeled in a cart with ice buckets and trays of foodstuffs.

"Champagne, gentlemen. And some dainties."

A corporal popped the cork on one of the bottles.

"A little too early for me, Hauptmann," Tom said. "No thanks."

"But I insist," the Prussian said pointedly, thrusting a champagne glass through the bars.

"Well, okay, if it makes you happy." Tom took the glass.

"It does, immensely," Hauptmann said as he poured.

Tom sampled the drink. "A very good year."

"One of the best. Mr. Brewster?"

"Oh, anytime's the time for me, old chap. Thank you so very much. My, that is good."

"And the good doctor."

"Thank you."

The other soldier was opening the cell door.

"Now if you gentlemen will follow me. Olam, I have something to show you. You were curious about our guidance system."

"Yes, very. What is it?"

"I will show you, Thomas, my good man. You don't mind if I call you Thomas, do you?"

"Would it matter?"

Laughing, Hauptmann led the way through a maze of dark corridors, column-left and column-right, until his unwilling troop, champagne cart bringing up the rear, came into a warren of rooms that looked like scientific laboratories, as indeed they were.

It was a room full of animal cages. There were a few rhesus monkeys and guinea pigs, but the bulk of the lab's inhabitants were birds. Pigeons, mainly.

White pigeons.

Long-delayed understanding dawned for Tom as Hauptmann explained.

"As you can see, these birds are specially trained. Namely, to peck at things. You see how this works—if they peck in the spot that's exactly correct, they get food. If they miss, or are the slightest bit off-target, they get nothing. Thus, accuracy is . . . how shall I put it . . . reinforced.

"You see the figure of the circle within a circle? It is a glass plate affair being projected by magic lantern. The smaller circle is centered on the cross hairs. If the rocket deviates from its prescribed flight path, the small circle drifts out from the cross hairs. This is the cue for the pigeon to set things right. Its pecking against the ground glass affects the Swiss clockwork mechanism that oversees the navigation of the ballistic rocket through its trajectory.

"The more the pigeon pecks, the more course correction is applied by the swiveling rocket nozzle. Very simple, you see. And we owe it all to these wonderful little creatures. Especially Henrietta, here. She is our best pecker." Hauptmann gently lifted the bird out of its training box and transferred her to her cage, where she immediately began drinking from a vial of water. "You get some rest, Henrietta. In an hour, you will fly as you have never flown before. Good girl. Drink up."

"Too bad you couldn't get one of our dwarf-size Babbage engines," Tom said.

"Yes, too bad. But this was always feasible as an alternative. When we ourselves devise a Babbage of the required size, which is only a matter of time, we will employ that for the KV-3. But we can hit almost any city with the pigeon method. Munich, included, of course. After all, cities are kilometers wide. With the K-3 and the Babbage guidance, however, we can hit a target the size of Castle Falkenstein dead on. Pinpoint."

"I must congratulate your engineers," Tom said.

"I will convey to them your admiration. Do have another glass of champagne, Olam."

"Thank you."

Tom stepped up to Henrietta's cage and bent over it, looking at the delicate creature. "Shame she has to die, poor girl."

"If it were within her power to choose, she would gladly give her life for the Fatherland. Now, gentlemen, I will escort you back to your own cage, as it were. And in just a short while, you will be conducted to your seats on the viewing stand. It's about a kilometer from the firing bed. No danger, if you're worrying."

"I love fireworks," Wynnie said.

"You are going to see the biggest rocket ever go up in glory," Hauptmann said.

"Good luck, Henrietta," Tom said as he passed Hauptmann, handing him an empty glass.

"She will succeed," Hauptmann said.

When they got back to the cell and were locked in, Hauptmann still was not done with them.

"I want your word as gentlemen that there will be no unseemly behavior at the ceremonies. Otherwise you will sit it out here."

"You have my word, Fritz, old kraut . . . sorry, Herr Hauptmann. And thanks awfully for the nice bubbly."

"Thank you, Mr. Brewster. Captain Olam, do I have your word as an officer and gentleman that you will be on your best behavior?"

"I give you my word."

"Mine, too," van Helsing said.

"Thank you. Very gracious of you, I must say. And now, gentlemen, if you'll forgive me, I have many last-minute duties to attend to."

Hauptmann clicked his heels, left-faced, and marched off.

The grandstand, constructed of green lumber, was a cheapjack structure, even for a temporary one. Hauptmann apparently never thought launches would become public events, as they would in another time and place, another universe. Of course, there was no television here, no radio. Only newspaper descriptions and the odd Daguerreotype would be available to the public at large, who weren't for the most part invited to this shindig. Those invited were mostly dignitaries, *Numero Uno* being, of course, the Chancellor, Otto von Bismarck.

Everybody in the grandstand rose at his arrival. He was not royalty, but many women curtsied, some men bowed. There he was, tall, powerfully built, almost ursine, with a bristling walrus mustache and a way of handling his body as if he were used to the world suiting him, rather than vice versa. When he spoke his voice rumbled with deep, powerful intonations.

Tom had seen him before, at Ludwig's coronation ball, where he had been polite to the king, charmed the ladies, and generally made an excellent impression, which in no way mitigated the fact that he was a threat to New Europa, wanting to cobble most of it up into a new German empire.

So here was the Iron Chancellor, and in one sense that was literal. His left arm was a clockwork prosthesis that he handled adroitly. You had to study its movements for a minute to tell that it was fake.

Hauptmann clomped up to Bismarck and presented himself, saluting crisply. Bismarck gave him a cursory return salute, then seated himself in the fancy wingback chair designated for him. After exchanging a few words with the young colonel, the Chancellor said curtly, "Get on with it."

Tom couldn't hear every word, seated as he was with Brewster and van Helsing off on the extreme left of the grandstand. He was half expecting a German band to come oom pahing in at any moment. But for all the flags and bunting draped over everything in sight, Tom didn't think Hauptmann would dare turn the affair into a circus. After all, this was a military-scientific test run.

And there was the rocket, standing on its fire bed out there on the beach, a click away, but tall and proud and very visible even without field glasses, smoke trailing out of its tail and rising into the sea-fresh morning air. The wind was calm, just a hint of a breeze. Good day to shoot off a rocket.

The guy has chutzpah, I'll give him that, Tom thought. Or maybe he has an Unseelie line into the future and already knows he has succeeded? No . . . not even the Unseelie could predict the future with any accuracy. They were too busy making it happen anyway.

"Tom? You have a call, old man," Brewster said, handing the cigarette case over.

"Marianne. Where are you now?"

Tom tried to understand the tiny image he perceived on the surface of the case. Marianne was there, he was sure, but she was standing behind Zambelli, who was seated in a chair in the middle of a room full of . . . what the hell was that?

"We are very near."

"Where?"

"We are circling Peenemünde. Where is the test site?"

" You have the magic mirror with you? I can't understand how you—"

"We're aboard the *Swanship Lohengrin*."

Tom did a take. "You're aboard . . . what?"

"The rocket. We call it the *Swanship Lohengrin*. You'll see. Or maybe not. I don't know yet. We're invisible at the moment."

Tom shook his head. "I go away for two weeks, and . . . Jeez, is that the control room?"

"The bridge."

"The *bridge?* What did you guys build, a spaceship?"

Marianne shrugged. "I thought that was the idea. Anyway, we are going to transport you aboard. Just stay where you are, and put the mirror somewhere so your reflection is in it."

"I have three to beam up . . . I don't believe I said that."

"Beam? What is beam? Oh, beam. Yes, fine, get them in the reflection. You understand?"

"I think. I still don't believe . . . ooops, Olam out."

"Who are you talking to?"

Tom gave the guard a wide grin. "Just practicing my ventriloquism."

The guard didn't buy it. "Shut up and be quiet. The ceremony is about to start."

"Herr Chancellor, ladies and gentlemen . . ."

Hauptmann, at the top of his lungs, launched into a windy speech about the glory of the Fatherland and other flourishes, but was cut embarrassingly short by a grunt from Bismarck, meaning, get on with it, and he meant, get on with it.

"Yes, Herr Chancellor!"

Hauptmann picked up a red signal flag and waved it to a man on a tower, who in turn relayed the signal down a line of towers to the fire control bunker, only about fifty meters from the rocket.

Tom was glad for the absence of any count-down routine. Just shoot the thing off. He was getting impatient.

There ensued about thirty seconds of delay between the last signal and the start of something on the fire bed. The rocket spat out a cloud of thick white smoke and began to rise, steadily, smoothly, confidently, into the bright blue sky.

Seconds later, the sound arrived, an ear-splitting roar like steady thunder combined with a rockslide or the collapse of a building. Ladies shrieked and covered their ears.

In moments the rocket was a silver and gold arrow in the sky, shooting heavenward but arching out to sea in a sure trajectory. It was a magnificent launch.

"I must say, that's a rum show," Brewster said dejectedly. "Looks like old Fritz pulled it off, eh? Blast."

"Van Helsing, lean over into the cigarette case, here," Tom instructed.

"What did you say, Tom?"

"Smile," Tom said, holding the cigarette case out to arms' length.

"Wait, something's happening."

Tom looked up and saw that the rocket's contrail had twisted a bit. Things all of a sudden didn't look so magnificent. People were rising from their seats and pointing. Exclamations went up.

"Damn thing's doubling back," Wynnie said.

"Holy hell," Tom said. "Uh, Wynnie, old chap—"

People were already up and running, screaming in fear. Others stuck to their seats in frozen terror.

"Jove's ballocks, the bloody thing's headed this way!"

Everybody hit the deck.

The rocket returned with lightning swiftness, slamming into the earth barely fifty meters from the grandstand, which promptly collapsed, not so much from the shock wave as from everyone's clumping toward the ends of it to get off. The explosion was tremendous, throwing up gouts of earth along with a flurry of instant scrap metal and a mushroom cloud of steam.

The debris never seemed to stop raining down. Finally, Tom dug himself out from under a pile of splintered fresh-cut timber and looked around. Wynnie and van Helsing were fine, it seemed. Tom looked around for the silver case.

Wynnie had it.

"Tom? Tom? Are you all right? My God, what went wrong?"

It was Marianne.

"Marianne, are you ready up there?"

"Yes, but I can't see three of you."

"Van Helsing, come here! Wynnie, step up. Hurry!"

Tom set the cigarette case up on a truncated stanchion, and they all linked arms as if posing for a picture.

"Energize!" Tom shouted.

Just before the strangeness started, Tom saw Hauptmann staggering up, his uniform torn and smudged, his proud Prussian spike bent. He looked a fright.

Hauptmann halted when he saw Tom. "*You!*"

Tom grinned. "I guess Henrietta couldn't hold her bubbly. Sorry. Oh, Rupert? One word. 'Autodestruct.' Think about it."

Hauptmann lunged, but he was brought up short by a strange thunder in the sky. He looked up and despaired.

Tom's eyes turned to saucers. Streaking across the test facility was a rocket ship out of Buck Rogers, trailing a stream of sparkling fire.

"What in the world is that?" Wynnie wanted to know.

Tom was about to hazard a guess, but right then the strangeness started.

CHAPTER 24

ROCKET TO MUNICH

The world flickered, then disappeared, replaced by something else. Without any sort of transition, Tom was standing, along with Brewster and van Helsing, atop a stage of sorts, in a cylindrical room. On the floor proper stood Marianne, smiling up at him. Beside her was Morrolan, of all people, standing at a console of some sort, pulling levers and things.

"Hello," Tom said.

Marianne jumped up on the stage and hugged him. "At last, you are safe. When that stupid rocket blew up I thought . . ."

"A miss as good as a mile, honey. Besides, I was the one who blew it up."

"You? How?"

"Oh, I got the pilot drunk."

"*Vraiment? Formidable!*"

"Nice work, old chap," Brewster said, shaking Tom's hand.

"Marianne," Tom said, "may I present Mr. Wyndham Brewster. And this is Dr. Abraham van Helsing. My partners in crime. Gentlemen, the Countess Marianne."

Van Helsing clicked his heels and kissed her hand. Brewster bowed.

"And now," Tom said, "may I ask . . . what the hell is all this?"

Morrolan stepped up. "This specifically, or—" he gestured about—"this?"

"How'd you do the matter transportation bit?"

"With a series of magic mirrors, that rack of prisms, these control cables, and . . . well, it's complex."

"Unbelievable," Tom said. "How do you get a three-dimensional image from a two-dimensional one?"

"Magic," Morrolan said.

"Right. Okay, where the hell are we? This is the rocket?"

"It's Zambelli's rocket, tricked up with some spiffy sorcerous engines," Marianne explained. "Well, that's how we started out. We crashed . . ."

"You crashed?"

"Yes, and the magic engines broke, but Zambelli's rocket works without them."

"And Zambelli's piloting it?"

Morrolan shrugged. "He volunteered. Rhyme was a little nervous about it. Let's give you the tour."

Tom saw the entire ship, including the engine room, where Rhyme was still busy trying to fix his sorcerous machine.

When he stepped into the control room, Tom couldn't believe his eyes. There was Zambelli in the pilot's seat. The ship was zooming over New Europa on the way back home, cruising like a jetliner with a quiet, steady roar of power.

"Where'd you learn to fly?" Tom asked.

"I'm wait all my life for this," Zambelli said with a satisfied grin. "And no devil stuff. The ship, she work. Eh?"

"She work," Tom said, then seated himself in one of the extra chairs. He strapped in.

Marianne was saying, "I think it was good that we lost the invisibility and showed the Prussians what we have. And everybody."

Tom shook his head. "Maybe. But I think it safe to say that the Prussian rocket program died today. If old Bismarck lived, he'll have Hauptmann's head on a platter. Anyway, even though people saw this thing today, if we lock it away and never fly it again, it will become a myth. No one will believe it."

"But they all saw with their own eyes," Tarlenheim said.

"Doesn't mean anyone seeing it would be believed. Take my word for it."

"It's all moot, anyway," Morrolan said. "No Prussian threat, no need for this infernal machine. I suggest we give it to the dwarfs."

"It's a shame," Tarlenheim said. "This is the mightiest warship that ever sailed the skies."

"Colonel," Marianne said, "it does not even have guns!"

Morrolan grinned at Tom. "We didn't have time to install any armaments."

"We wanted, you know, to make *la tour de force*, but the Prussians, they scared themselves."

"Still seems a shame," Tarlenheim said. "But I suppose it is for the best. I never was one for machines in war. War is not for machines, it is for men."

"Besides," Morrolan said, "building a fleet of these would be problematical. Too much magic to handle."

"It is for the best," Tom said. "Rockets don't belong in the nineteenth century. At least not the twenty-first century kind."

And so the *Lohengrin* came home to Castle Falkenstein, where it went into hover mode and set down in the central courtyard on legs of fire. The castle emptied, its staff and inhabitants pouring out to greet the aeronauts, cheering wildly. Despite the secrecy, word of mouth had kept the servants informed about Zambelli's rocket ship. It is difficult to keep any secret from the staff of any castle, and Castle Falkenstein was no different in this regard.

"It really does look like something out of Flash Gordon!" Tom marveled once he got to see the outside of the thing.

"Flash who?" everyone chorused.

"Never mind."

Ludwig was there to greet everyone, expressing his appreciation. He was informed at once about the cessation of the Prussian rocket threat, and this made him almost deliriously happy.

"Well, I must say," he exclaimed, "this calls for a royal feast. We shall have the finest ever at Falkenstein. Music, dancing, food, everything. Let's go back inside, though, there's a chill."

On his way in, Tom caught sight of Auberon.

"Hey, I've a few bones to pick with you."

"I suppose you do," Auberon said with a wry smile.

"What was the big idea of dumping me into the Prussians' hands?"

"I had a number of reasons. The primary one being the difficulty of moving a doorway to the Veil. The secondary one was that your quest was not completed. You were not yet at the end of that path, the path I spoke about the night of the ball."

"Say . . . you rescued Goethe, didn't you? The night of the ball?"

"Goethe? Oh, you mean the man with the knife in his chest? Well, Tom, in a way I did. I saw him dying and was compelled to help. As the damage had been done with magic, I could undo it easily, reversing time just a smidge and altering a few things. He was perfectly fine after that. Nevertheless, he was frightened out of his wits and fled. Did it upset your plans very much?"

"No, just caused some confusion. So he was legit after all, and the Prussians were on to him. I hope he got away."

"I'm sure he did," Auberon said. "Any other bones?"

"None. Thanks, Auberon."

"Glad to help."

Just as everyone began crowding through the big doors of the castle, there came shouts from behind. Tom whirled and looked.

The ship was rising on its pillars of flame again.

"Who's aboard that craft?" Tarlenheim shouted.

"Zambelli!"

"Oh, no, the mad fool."

The *Lohengrin* whooshed away into the sky, became a dot against the blue, then vanished. A full moon hung in the east.

"Three guesses where he's going," Morrolan said.

"The madman. Well, that's that." Tarlenheim straightened his uniform and marched indoors.

"But his wife and children," Marianne said.

"He'll be back," Tom said. "I have a feeling."

EPILOGUE

"Goethe" escaped from Prussia, emigrated to America, and went to work for a company that devised and manufactured parlor games for adults.

Otto von Bismarck made a quick recovery from superficial injuries, and went back to the business of building the German empire.

Rupert Hauptmann was relieved of his commission, and demoted to corporal. He was given a revolver and left alone in his quarters, but he declined to do the manly thing. He spent his remaining years serving in a regiment of Prussian infantry stationed near the Danish border. His duties included latrine detail.

Moriarty, later known as Professor Moriarty, for he was a brilliant man, went on to become one of the leading criminals of New Europa, winning the Nebulous award for conspicuous villainy, yearly given by the Society for the Furthering of World Anarchy.

Abraham van Helsing took his doctorate of philosophy from the Sorbonne, and wrote a dissertation on the legends of the living dead, concentrating on vampires. He was often quoted as saying that it was a subject one could get one's teeth into.

Captain Nemo continued his undersea quest for the kraken. Later, he underwent psychoanalysis in Vienna.

Wyndham Brewster found Castle Falkenstein an absolutely ripping place to spend the weekend, and spent many of them there over the next few years. His man, Slope, accompanied him. Slope allowed that the place was not without its Teutonic charm, if one cared for that sort of thing.

Ruggiero Zambelli did return, in fact, a week later, walking out of a mirror in his quarters in the castle. No one saw him do this. Not even his wife, who was busy in the kitchen at the time, watching Berenice roll out pasta dough. When he showed up at a castle soiree that night, he burst forth with a story about how he had landed on the surface of the moon, but could not for the life of him open the main hatch. Soon, he began to have trouble breathing. He suspected that there was no air on the moon. No air, at all. And no water to run the boilers for the magical engines. Which is why he had to leave the ship there and fiddle with the mirror transporter until it spirited him back to the castle. Which made him uneasy, for he did not like to fool with the devil's magic.

No one believed a word he said. Nevertheless, he returned to Italy a fulfilled man, having realized a lifelong dream. He has no intention of ever going back to the moon, nor of traveling the black reaches of outer space. It seems that, once you do it, it scratches the itch, and you are freed to return to earthly concerns.

Auberon and his Seelie carried on their struggle against the machinations of the Adversary and his Unseelie hosts. The matter is still very much up in the air.

Tom Olam and Marianne continued to live in Castle Falkenstein, happily having many more wonderful adventures. And if you are good children, I will tell you about more of them.

Other Proteus Books
Now Available from Prima!

The 7th Guest: A Novel $21.95
Matthew J. Costello and Craig Shaw Gardner

In the 1st Degree: A Novel $19.95
Dominic Stone

X-COM UFO Defense: A Novel $5.99
Diane Duane

Celtic Tales: Balor of the Evil Eye—A Novel $5.99
Aaron Conners

The Pandora Directive: A Tex Murphy Novel $5.99
Aaron Conners

Hell: A Cyberpunk Thriller—A Novel $5.99
Chet Williamson

**Wizardry: The League of the Crimson Crescent
—A Novel** $5.99
James Reagan

Star Crusader—A Novel $5.99
Bruce Balfour

To Order Books

Please send me the following items:

Quantity	Title	Unit Price	Total
_____	_____	$ _____	$ _____
_____	_____	$ _____	$ _____
_____	_____	$ _____	$ _____
_____	_____	$ _____	$ _____
_____	_____	$ _____	$ _____
_____	_____	$ _____	$ _____

Subtotal	$ _____
7.25% Sales Tax (CA Only)	$ _____
8.25% Sales Tax (TN Only)	$ _____
5.0% Sales tax (MD only)	$ _____
7.0% G. S. T. Canadian Orders	$ _____
Shipping and Handling*	$ _____
Total Order	$ _____

*\$4.00 shipping and handling charge for the first book and \$1.00 for each additional book.

By telephone: With MC or Visa, call (916) 632-4400 Mon.-Fri., 9-4 PST.

By mail: Just fill out the information below and send with your remittance to:

Prima Publishing
P.O. Box 1260BK
Rocklin, CA 95667

Satisfaction unconditionally guaranteed

Name _____

Street _____ Apt. _____

City _____ State _____ Zip _____

MC/Visa # _____ Exp. _____

Signature _____

About the Author

John DeChancie is the author of numerous popular fantasy novels that remain perennially in print! His works include The Kruton Interface series, Bride of the Castle, Castle Dreams, Castle Spellbound, and co-authorship of Dr. Dimension: Masters of Spacetime.